Something in your Eyes

Smiling in the sky…

Something in your Eyes

Smiling in the sky...

Saikat Baksi

Srishti
PUBLISHERS & DISTRIBUTORS

Srishti Publishers & Distributors
N-16, C. R. Park
New Delhi 110 019
srishtipublishers@gmail.com

First published by Srishti Publishers & Distributors in 2009
6th impression, 2011

Typeset in AGaramond 11pt. by Suresh Kumar Sharma at Srishti

Printed and bound in India

To

The invisible force that propelled me into the thick of life

From the backstage...

One fine morning after four years of my birth, I wrote few words and called that a poem! My mother was convinced that her child would turn out to be a legendary poet some day! From that morning onwards I never stopped writing and painting.

My father, in spite of having the capability of becoming one of the finest dramatists of his time, ended up devoting his passion to building his son's future. Even today, his prime goal in life is to see his son as a successful writer.

They injected inspirations that ran with unbridled fervour in my veins.

I am indebted to my wife who relieved me of almost every household duty. Without this, it would have been very difficult for me to pursue my passion as well as do justice to my professional responsibilities as a corporate executive. My daughter's belief that her father is a great man boosts my resolve to attain greater height. My little boy's exuberance reminds me that life has just started...long way to go.

I am extremely obliged to Jayantada for recognising the goodness in my work.

I want to live in this very world for a thousand years and narrate all the stories I have and I shall have.

Finally, I am thankful to life that gifted me more than I asked for.

It's another day

The large framed man with neatly carved beard and a pair of expensive sunglasses snugly set on his slightly large but blunt nose drove into the parking area of the food mall. The swanky food mall by the side of the highway was situated adjacent to a petrol pump. The highway stretched infinitely in both directions cuddled by wilderness shriveled under the merciless glare of midday sun. The concrete road looked like a venomous snake wrapped around the poisoned earth stretching from one horizon to the other.

He was hungry as well as frustrated. This hundred-and-eighty-kilometer stretch connecting two major cities ran through arid lands and wild mountains. The dark brown mounds raised their ominous massive heads which solemnly towered over the thin winding concrete road. Sometimes the road looked rather delicate with respect to the rugged vastness under the deep blue sky. Blistering heat of summer singed every object exposed under the sky; but still there were trees and bushes as well as layers of grass which adamantly held on to their residual pale greenness. They sizzled but did not give up breathing. The pale struggling leaves gaped lifelessly at the smug and audacious sun hoping for better days. And...indeed better days always emerged from the glaring heat waves...every year better days emerged...it was just a matter of lasting till they emerged.

There was a cluster of petrol pumps and eating joints every forty kilometers span along the highway. The slogging and sweltering engines as well as stomachs were taken care of in these roadside clusters. After a halt of half an hour on an average to brace the gasping spirit, they dashed away along the concrete highway once again.

As he was adjusting the orientation of his massive car, the cell phone started ringing with a start. He bent his head to check the caller and immediately picked up the phone in a hurry as if another second's delay in responding to the call would decide life and death.

"Hi…so…are you okay now? Feeling stronger? Just woke up?" He said trying to sound calm but his voice betrayed his effort.

"Where the hell are you?"

"Well…look…I was there by the side of your bed till twelve in the morning. Seeing your face I felt that you were recovering quickly. The deathly pallor was gone and it was full of life although you were sound asleep then."

"Come on…don't talk in riddles. Have you deserted me? Talk straight."

"Ahh…you don't understand…I did not leave you for ever…I have an extremely urgent work to attend to and I will be back in say another two days. Till then you will surely recover completely. Your kitchen is fully stuffed with all kinds of fruits and other stuff. Don't worry at all. When I come back two days later, we can then…"

"Don't give me that crap. I have heard all that many times from you. You just left me at large to rot alone. You are running to that bloody bitch; the bitch that you call your wife. You are nothing more than a spineless prick, you know."

"You are misunderstanding me. It's not my wife I am running for. I told you that I have some extremely urgent work that I must attend to."

"Tell me! What is that work?"

"Well..."

"That bitch wants to sleep with you right now? She can't wait?"

"Oh! You are impossible. It's my son's admission in school and they want to interview the parents. I have to be there tomorrow morning. I have no choice."

"Hmm...I see. I can understand ... either it's a ploy of that slut or it's you who has built the story...but what can I do! Nothing!" She started sobbing convulsively.

"Please...please try to understand ... I am not going away or anything...it's just a few days and I shall be back. In this condition of health you are advised to avoid any kind of excitement. Please don't cry."

"What is it that I have? You tell me...a kitchen full of fruits? A nice apartment with marble floor and a host of expensive furniture? A car waiting at the parking lot? And...and? What?"

"What else do you want? Name it and I shall make it yours. What have I not done for you till date? And still you gulped those sleeping pills!"

"Why? Don't you know what I want? I spit on this house and the car...take them away...I don't want them. I want you to marry me and leave that baggage behind. But you are not doing it. You are a coward and a greedy animal. You want both. You want your cushy doting home with that bitch in it and at the same time you want a beautiful young woman stashed somewhere two hundred kilometers away as a mistress so that you can use her for your carnal satisfaction as and when you want. Right? But no! I am not going to let it happen. You will either marry me or I shall destroy your tender and pristine home...do you understand?"

He was silent for a long moment and then said "Can we talk after say one hour? I am waiting in the middle of the parking lot oddly blocking the movement of other vehicles...please try to understand."

She snapped the line abruptly.

He threw the cell phone on the empty seat in frustration and pulled the back gear to adjust the position of the car. He started reconsidering his plan of spending two nights at home. It was indeed the interview at the school for admission of his four-year-old son. The school management was hell bent on having a chat with the parents before admitting the child. He could not help but attend the same. Only ... may be he will have to conjure up another excuse for coming back by next evening itself. Otherwise things would go beyond control. While he was gathering his purse and cigarette packet, a man walking past his car suddenly stopped and pointed his finger at the front left wheel. He looked at the man quizzically anticipating the most unwelcome trouble. The man swept his palm horizontally in the air indicating that the front left tyre of his car was flattened. He took a deep breath and cast a resigned look in a general direction into the dry and sizzling horizon. This was the last piece of ill luck that could have befallen him. He turned off the engine which died smoothly with a mild tremble as if finally exhaustion took hold of its overstretched muscles. He still did not move but sat inside the car with a comatose mind. He knew that he needed to do some active thinking but could not inject any stimulus of life into the immobile numbness. The air-conditioner was not on and the blower quickly started throwing a hot blast of air on his face. It became impossible to sit any further inside the closed space of the car. He clambered out of the car and lifelessly walked towards the front left wheel with the hope that his interpretation of the man's gesture was mistaken; but no!

The front left tyre was totally deflated and appeared to be in a pretty damaged condition. Almost all the threads were smoothed out. It had rubbed against the hard surface of the road for quite a distance it seemed.

He stared at the tyre for a long moment and then concluded that he had no way other than getting it repaired. Slowly his mind started getting back its composure. "First let me have some food, then I shall take care of this matter," he thought aloud.

Locking the car, he walked up to the eating area.

"One grilled fish combo with extra cheese."

"Hundred and five rupees, Sir."

"Oh...please add one more slice of cheese with the burger."

"You will get extra cheese anyway."

"I know what your extra cheese version is. I want one more in that slab."

"Sorry! That's not our standard. I can't offer you something special like that...you can take a cheese dip along with it."

"I said another additional cheese slice in the burger! It's not cheese dip."

"But I can't make an entry in the system for such a request. Please try to understand."

"I am ready to pay...what is the problem!"

"Sorry, sir. I am helpless."

"Ridiculous! I have money...I pay for this additional cheese slice but you will not give me!"

The clerk at the counter kept silent asserting his stand.

He twitched his face in anger and threw a hundred-rupee note and a coin on the desk. The coin hit the granite surface and, after bouncing once, it rolled over the desk to finally fall on the ground.

The clerk glared at this show of insolence and bent down to the ground to find the coin. He kept looking for the coin and could not find the metal object anywhere on the floor. After a few minutes the clerk reappeared in front of the desk without the coin and peevishly said, "Sorry, sir, I could not find it. You have to give me another coin."

He snapped, "What? Another coin! Nonsense! I shall not give you a farthing. You search it out later and now give me the burger and other things that I ordered."

The clerk stood adamantly. "I can not. The price is hundred and five rupees including tax and I have received only hundred. I want the remaining five and then only you will get your Grill-fish combo. Is that clear?"

Suddenly his fuse was blown and he muttered under his breath, "You bloody waiter! How dare you talk to me like that? You are not even worth a single penny, and you are fighting for five rupees! Here! Take... take this! Take hundred...two hundred...three hundred! How much do you want? Take it." Screaming hysterically, he pulled out three hundred-rupee notes and threw them on the face of the clerk.

The clerk did not react but simply turned and picked up one burger, one cold drink and a small packet of French fries. He arranged them on the tray along with the three hundred-rupee notes miserably crumpled and placed the tray on the desk.

He fumed in anger and grabbed the tray after keeping aside the notes on the granite platform. Before leaving the counter he sneered, "Keep the change."

He walked out of the air conditioned enclosure of the counter and stepped into the hot sun again. It was one of those extremely hot days in summer. There was an open air lawn with an overhead shed to protect the area from direct sunlight, on which chairs and tables were sprawled all over. He chose to sit at the centre to stay away from the scorching heat as well as to keep him out of the sight of the counter where the clerk would be standing.

He unwrapped the burger and started eating the succulent slabs of soft bread, fried fish and molten cheese smeared with mayonnaise. The open space was located next to a large stretch of barren land which finally raised itself to form a mound of stone and dry soil dotted with pale green shrubs.

Hot wind hurtled down the slanting surface of the hillock and tried to sweep away everything on its way. He was finding it difficult to keep the paper pack of French fries in place. Twice the packet was almost on its way to join the journey with the blowing wind. There were many other people taking a break, refueling their spirit as well as their vehicles. The aura was supposed to be of relaxation but instead the hollow dryness instilled a feeling of hopeless lethargy in the air. The dazzling glare of the sun forced everyone to stare at the horizon with their eyes squeezed to allow less whiteness within the limit of tolerance. The concrete road ahead appeared like a formidable challenge straining the nerves of the onlookers even before restarting their journey.

He ate his food while reflecting back on his life. He would have to call her back anyway. Any default on that would further complicate his life. In fact, he wanted to call.

She gulped a handful of sleeping pills three days before! Why did she do that? Well, he knew the answer. It's good that she survived; otherwise, his life would already have been completely ruined. But... but what could have stopped that? Nothing! He bought enough luxury for her but that was not enough. What else did she want? Even his wife did not enjoy so much of material pleasure as she did over last four years. He believed one thing for sure— that money could buy anything... just anything...starting from a burger to love. Prices varied...that was all! It was just a matter of who could afford what. It was only lately that he was slightly confused about handling her needs. As for himself, his wants were well defined. He wanted thrill, sex and romance which were simply missing at home. A ten-year-old marriage resulted in a brooding wife and a naughty kid. He loved his son though. He could afford to stay at home barely one or two days a week but whenever he returned home he carried some expensive gift for his son. He was certain that the toys would definitely substitute his physical presence.

It was not exactly like this before, when his business was growing in leaps and bounds and his marriage was fresh. His wife was a happy soul and they used to enjoy doing things together during the weekends as well as in the remaining few hours of the evening on weekdays at home. The business was rewarding him with loads of money and he was becoming almost rich. One day, the old man who acted as his personal secretary in the company left his job due to poor health and he needed to recruit someone in his place. He interviewed several candidates but the attractive dusky young lady with large round eyes and unruly curves stung his sensuality without warning. He at once recruited her as his personal secretary. She came from a small town and had barely any relative in the city. She needed money badly and actually lacked requisite qualities for getting a decent white-collar job. He appointed her quickly for taking care of his affairs in office. But from the very first day of her arrival in the office, his senses were tantalized wildly. He analyzed the situation quickly. He understood that she did not have many more decent options but to be on the job. The salary was not exorbitant but that was the lifeline for her. His roving eyes penetrated every visible inch of her physical beauty during any interaction between them. One fine evening he hinted about his hidden desires. Also, along with that, he suggested a significant salary hike from that month itself. She submitted to this bargain. And that's how it all started. Slowly his complete' carnal desires were shifted to his secretary whereas his family started looking redundant. She learnt soon that he might have started that affair as a mere barter system, a mechanical exchange of practical favors to each other, but at some point, his mind also started meddling between them. He started to fall in love with her. And that's when she decided to up her bargains. She hinted at leaving the job and going away. He was alarmed. By then she was really groomed as a smart and charming personality. She could easily get another job. He did not waste any time but suggested that she should leave her dingy ladies hostel and shift to a rented apartment in a posh locality in the city. She did it and he paid the rental. In the wake of this romantic venture, only trouble loomed in the horizon when other employees in the office felt the pinch of being neglected whereas she enjoyed all the privileges. In fact her apparent high-handed behavior with other employees caused ample number of disgruntled colleagues. As it always happened, her being beautiful and attractive also drew attention of other young employees in the organization but they had to stay away at an arms-length distance to avoid attracting the wrath of the boss. One day, one such employee left the company on a bitter note and went straight to his house to apprise his wife about the shameful debauchery he was indulging in.

That was a stormy evening for him as he came back home. In the following days his wife became extremely vigilant about his daily affairs and one morning rushed to his office to sound a deathly warning about the terrifying consequences if there was any damage to her married life.

After all these, he decided that the whole affair must switch to another route. It was not really important that she worked for him in the office. She could simply resign from the job on the pretext of that embarrassing rumour and disappear out of the sight of the employees of this organization. They would believe that the whole story was over anyway. On the other hand he could settle her in another city some two hundred kilometers away where he would purchase her a nice apartment and install an expensive car at the basement for her service. He would visit her on the pretext of his business on a regular basis. The whole thing would be pretty safe and secured.

All was well and events moved in the direction as expected till the time when one fine day she realized that she would run out of her physical charm some time in the future and he would run away from her. Perhaps he would be back to his family as before.

In spite of a million reassurances she was not convinced and she could find only one solution to the whole problem. That was marriage.

She started insisting that he should leave his wife and child for ever and marry her. In fact, she wanted a baby as well. He was at a loss when this request was put up in front of him. It was never his consideration at all. He tried to push aside the idea by distracting her with various kinds of material pleasures. But they worked only temporarily and soon she was back on her track. She wanted him to marry her and snap all the old ties.

And it was then that she gulped a handful of sleeping pills in a fit of frenzy while fighting with him. Luckily , she survived unhurt and when she was sound asleep after three days, he got a call from his wife that he must be back home for their child's admission the next morning. He left for home keeping a small note for her that he would come back shortly.

He swallowed the last crumb of the burger left on the tray and unmindfully kept chewing the straw of the cold drink. Finishing his food he stood under the shade for a few minutes lingering over the idea of stepping into the blistering sun to look for a tyre repair shop. He walked up to a guard and asked, "Do you know any place here to repair a punctured tyre?"

Pat came the reply, "Yes, it is right behind the petrol pump."

The guard indicated, "See…there is that large red signboard…exactly behind the signboard you will find him. You better call him and he will come here to take your tyre for repair."

He thanked him and started contemplating his next move. The signboard seemed some three hundred meters away from where he was at the moment and if he would have to call the fellow he would have to walk right through this hell fire of heat. Instead he could simply drive his car down slowly up to where the shop was. Finally, he reasoned if the car could run at hundred kilometers per hour with this punctured condition for so many kilometers, why could it not take another quarter of a kilometer. No significant harm anyway.

He sat behind the wheel and started driving it carefully towards the repair shop.

The shed

It was a small shed made of scrapped sheets of tin and covered with cheap tarpaulin over a flimsy skeleton of bamboo. In fact it was outside the wall of the petrol pump, shyly occupying a small section of the wide barren stretch. The man of around thirty years was lying huddled on a shabby bed and a boy of around twelve years sat on the ground fiddling with a dirty greasy half of a gearbox. The man seemed to be half asleep. There was a fan that ran on illegal electric connection drawn from the petrol pump. The fan swung violently from one side to the other as it rotated throwing a blast of hot air all over the place.

He watched the repair shop from inside the car for some time. Piles of rejected tyres arranged one above the other carelessly outside the shed blocked a clear view but he was sure that there were some people inside. Instead of going out of the car, he pressed the horn. After sounding the roaring horn thrice, it seemed that the man lying on the bed suddenly sat up with a jerk and asked the boy to check what the driver of the car wanted.

The boy ran out of the shed and appeared in front of the car. He lowered the tinted glass of the window and said, "The front left tyre is punctured."

The boy nodded his head in assurance that the solution could be provided and ran back to the shed to inform the man who was now standing and was craning his head to find out more.

The boy went back and reported the situation. The man pulled out a plastic bottle from one corner of the shed and poured some water on his palm to splash the same on his face. Then he walked out to get near the car.

Seeing the man approaching he stepped out of the car and tried to speak aloud, "Look at this one. It's deflated totally. I guess it's punctured."

The man did not answer. He always wondered why people narrated their problems in words every time they arrived at his shed. Since he could only repair tyres, it's obvious that one would come to him for tyre repair only. He took a quick glance at the wheel and gestured to the boy to bring the tools for jacking the car up. He watched the man indifferently.

"How long will it take?" he asked.

"Let me see the tyre closely. It seems you have driven in this condition quite a long distance," said the man.

"I want it done fast. I have no time."

The man was now inspecting the tyre closely sitting on his knee on the concrete surface.

He had seen thousands of tyres in his life over these past twenty years. In fact he had seen more tyres than human faces. The repair shop had a strange aura of dynamism for him. Every visitor came there just to go away as quickly as possible. And, this was not limited to the customers only but even the wild wind always came to visit him from somewhere across the mountains and left in a hurry. Wind spoke to him when nobody was there with him except the boy. The boy knew that the wind spoke to him. In fact the boy also often tried to take part in the conversation but could not decipher the dialogues.

The petrol pump adjacent to the shed had been there for a long time but the ownership changed hands a number of times and along with that the employees. Hence no body knew who the man was, where he came from and where he was destined to go. The boy was equally anonymous. Well, they were anonymous to others but known to each other and the reckless wind and the wilderness.

The man never bothered about his own origin. The earlier owner of the repair shop one day happened to ask a wandering boy to stay and work with him. He stayed and learned to work on the damaged tyres. Over fifteen years of stay with the earlier owner, he never encountered one visitor who came in search for him. Hence he became convinced over time that he belonged to the aimlessly blowing wind and whimsically sprawling sunlight because they specifically came to visit him all over the year. In fact rain also paid occasional visits to him but rain perhaps had other engagements elsewhere too and hence could show up only once a year. When the earlier owner left the place for some reason, he handed over the shed along with the crude equipments to the man for running the business. The man took charge. By that time he knew how to change tyres and also, with difficulty, how to count money. He hated money because he had seen that money had no mind of its own but stuck to the chest of whoever grabbed it. Money was not a free soul like the wind or the sun or the rain. He held money with disdain. The boy also seemed to have a similar fate in the sense that he too had no possessive owner. One day a truck came there for repair and the boy came along with that. When the tyres of the truck were ready, the boy was wandering across the barren land and the driver as well as the helper could not locate him. They left without him. As the boy came back the truck was missing. So, the man offered the boy a living in lieu of doing small errands when necessary.

The man unfastened the bolts and carefully pulled out the tyre from the hub.

"Could you move a little fast? You seem to have all the time in the world."

"Let me do my job. This tyre does not seem to be in a good shape," the man said to him.

He stared at the man with knitted brows and squinted eyes. The dazzling glow of the sun was too intense to keep his eyes wide open. As he breathed, hot air gushed through his nostrils and filled the gasping lungs. Suddenly, his cell phone started ringing. He checked the caller for few seconds and could not identify the source. Finally he received the call.

"What is happening to my consignment?"

He quickly realized who the caller was and flinched in irritation "Oh! Your consignment is on its way."

"I have been hearing that from your people for the past ten days and it is just a one-day journey by road. So, stop giving me that crap. Tell me the truth."

"I don't quite like the way you are speaking to me."

"I don't care what you like or dislike. I want my consignment."

"It's with the transporter. You know your consignment was not large enough to form a full truckload and hence the truck had to wait for several days before consolidation of consignments for different clients."

"I don't believe that piece of information. It could be three days or at the most four or five days but not beyond that. Why don't you give me the contact detail of the transporter? I shall myself find out what the matter is."

"I can't give you that right now. I am stuck somewhere in the middle of the road. You will get all the details by tomorrow morning."

"Well, then you are refusing to share this information. What do you think? I can't find out? I paid all the money for the goods in advance and now you are making up stories and lame excuses! I shall not spare you ... remember."

"Do whatever you want. If you speak like that, better don't talk to me." He snapped the line in anger.

The man was trying to set the tyre onto the fixture while beads of sweat glistened on his forehead.

He took a look at the tyre-less front of the car held up by the jack and started pondering what should be his next move to tackle that impending trouble. Finally he dialed his office number.

"What has happened to the consignment?"

"No idea! It left our premises nine days ago and is still with the transporter."

"Get me the number of the transporter."

He noted down the number on his palm and was about to disconnect the line. The voice on the other end said, "Sir, one pressing issue is there. Can I describe that?"

He answered in a flustered tone, "Carry on. Fast. I am also in the middle of a crisis."

"Sir, you had been briefed about that workman who was gathering immense popularity among the workers."

"Yes...what about him?"

"The workers are planning to stage a protest against the poor salary structure under his leadership."

"Hmm...how critical it is?"

"It's very critical. He is causing agitation in the factory."

"I think you should immediately hold a discussion with him."

"But...what do we discuss. All decisions are in your hand. You are not in office. They want a decision."

"Oh! I am giving you the decision right now."

"Yes sir!"

"Promote him from worker grade to officer grade. Increase his salary and perks to that of a middle level executive. That way he will be able to only sympathize but not lead them."

"That's right. Thanks! We shall do that."

He snapped the line and checked his palm if the writing was wiped off due to sweat. It was there intact.

"Why don't you come under the shade? It's cool over here," the man said addressing him while adjusting the lever against the alloy rim.

He looked at the shabby interior of the shed sneeringly and contemplated if he should accept the invitation. In first place he never believed that it would be cool inside the shed. The shed was not air conditioned. Only a splash of chilled air could console his burning skin; and that would have been possible only if he was sitting inside his car with the air-conditioner blown to its fullest power. But this was not possible at the moment. Finally he concluded that he should better stay under the shade at least to avoid the direct sun.

He carefully walked along the narrow dusty opening between the petrol pump wall and the heap of stone and scraps. His shoes were polished like a mirror and were reflecting the ruthless rays of sun. He took each step with caution so as not to soil the polished shoe.

Once inside the shed, the boy quickly dragged a metallic box from somewhere and indicated him to seat himself comfortably. He waved his hand in dismissal and kept standing resolutely while trying the number of the transporter.

There was a response at the transporter's office.

"What happened to your truck? Or it's a bullock cart?"

"It's very unfortunate. The truck met with an accident on its way and the whole thing is actually toppled across the divider blocking half of the road on both sides."

"You know what…I care a fuck about the misfortune of your truck. I want my consignment to reach the destination in another three hours time."

"That's absurd. You can claim insurance."

"But my client will not get the material if I get insurance."

"But sir, please try to understand that this is an accident. No one intended this and this has not happened due to any negligence on our part. I am sure your client would understand the situation."

"I don't want to understand all that. I simply want my material to be taken out of that debris and carried by whatever means possible … by helicopter…by horse … by…by anything… In a nutshell all the cartons should be at my client's warehouse before seven o' clock this evening…that's it."

"It's impossible and absurd."

"I shall pay anything…make it happen."

"There is no way."

"I shall pay in advance. Tell me the amount and send some one to my office. The money will be ready."

"Oh! No amount of money can do the job."

In the height of frustration he hung up.

Immediately his phone started ringing once again. It was the irate client.

"I am canceling your order."

"Please listen…the truck met with an accident…"

"I am not interested. By the way, your company is blacklisted. No business ever in future!"

"Please…you can deduct the liquidity damage charges…"

"That will not cover one percent of my financial damage and reputation. The ship is scheduled to leave the port day after tomorrow and I am still waiting for your consignment."

"Okay…whatever financial damage you incur, you can pass it on to me."

"You seem to have forgotten that reputation cannot be purchased by money. Good bye."

He kept holding the phone for some more time against his ear although the line was disconnected already.

The man removed the rubber tube from the tyre and pumped air into the same. The tube swelled quickly but started oozing out air through several openings across the surface of the tube. The man made a gesture of disapproval and carried the tube to a dirty tub which was full of water. As he kept dipping different parts of the tube into the water, bubbles came rushing out like a fizz from several points.

"This tube is totally destroyed in heat. Also you have been driving in this condition for a long time, I guess. You must change the tube," declared the man.

"How much would it cost? Do you have an original company made tube or all spurious material?"

"Four hundred. It's not original. An original would cost you more."

He was visibly irritated. "I don't drive a truck or a delivery van. I put only original company made tubes. You are not going to fit a spurious tube there."

The man was at a loss. He left the deflated tube in the tub and walked towards him while wiping his face with the back of his hand. "But this is what I have."

He muttered angrily. "I don't like cheap stuff and that's what I have to use now. What else can I do? Go ahead and, by the way…let me see if I have these four hundred with me…I guess it's a thousand…can you give me the change?"

He took out his wallet to check if he had four hundred rupee notes and slowly his face wore an anxious expression. All the confidence seemed to drain out of his demeanor.

The man was taking out a plastic packet from under the bed. He silently rifled through the notes and bills neatly arranged inside his wallet and in a fit of anxiety slowly sat on the tin basket. Immediately he realized that his expensive clothes would get marks of grease and he sprang up in reflex action.

Hesitantly, he mumbled, "I have a problem here. Do you think I could find an ATM around?"

The man looked at him curiously.

"An ATM …I have only two hundred-rupee notes left in my wallet. I forgot to withdraw money…" he repeated.

The man started laughing. "It's a highway. You can see plenty of dry barren land, even some bushes as well as hillocks here and there…but no ATM for sure. Since I don't need much money, I never went in search of such a machine. By the way, how much do you have?"

He hesitantly stated. "Two hundred. But I can pay you the balance in another hour's time. There is a small town fifteen kilometers off this highway. I shall definitely find an ATM there. But the only way for me to get there is in my car. So, if you do the repair first, I can take my car, withdraw the money and pay you the balance in an hour's time…is that okay?"

The man was still smiling. "Don't get anxious. Loss of two hundred rupees is bearable for me. I told you I did not need much money."

"For the last two days, he is eating very little. So, we need no money practically. The food mall offers their excess food to me almost free of cost," the boy intercepted.

He was rather surprised at this strange response and remarked rather oddly. "Not eating much!"

The man smiled again. "That's the heat, you know. It's too tough lately. Also, something very strange happens here in the early morning...say around three onwards. It gets very cold actually. But during the whole day this hot sun and dry wind are somehow taking away all the hunger from the stomach."

He eventually thought over his own hunger and felt that he was becoming thirsty and hungry again. The whole conversation looked totally absurd to him.

He did not speak any more and decided that he would anyway take the diversion and withdraw some money to pay the remaining two hundred rupees to this man once the car was ready.

"You carry on your job. I will be back in five minutes. Do you think I can get some cold drink in that petrol pump or I shall have to go all the way to the food mall?"

The man thought for a while and answered in a tone of resignation that he never tried to find one in the petrol pump, neither in the food plaza. He motioned to the boy to bring the plastic bottle which was hidden somewhere in the shed. The boy fetched the bottle which contained some liquid in it, hot to the extent of boiling point.

"You can have some water from that. It's not cold but a better choice for you than walking that distance under the sun," said the man.

He did not reply but started to walk towards the mall and exactly at that moment he received a call from her. He almost jumped from the ground realizing that he was supposed to call back. He quickly did a calculation about how he would tackle the issue; but considering the sensitivity of the situation he decided to stay where he was. Walking in the scorching heat would deactivate his calculative mind. He remained in the shed.

"Hi! It's too hot out here."

"Yes I know it's hot. Did you call me to discuss the weather?"

"Let's discuss a little. At the moment that's the subject on top of my mind."

"Well, not on top of my mind. When are you coming back? I want you tomorrow afternoon. We have to sort it out."

"That we can sure do but don't you think that this summer is too hard for your beautiful skin?"

"What are you trying to say?"

"Nothing serious...just wondering how would it be like in Switzerland at the moment...you know ...those snowcapped mountains...a cute cottage on the edge of the slopping hill...clouds floating into the rooms...you and me! How is that?"

"Meaning?"

"Meaning...you and me are going to Switzerland in another ten days time."

She screamed in ecstasy. "Oh, my God! Really! In another ten days! But... but...I have no winter clothing...what about the Visa...?"

"Everything will be organized. Don't worry. I shall work out the Visa and we shall do the shopping for your garments as I come back within two days."

"All right. I don't know. Sometimes it seems you really love me. Okay...you are free for two days."

"That's all fine but how do you feel now?"

"I am fine. As if I never had those pills."

"Good! Now let me hang up. I am taking care of a punctured tyre in my car."

"I told you to change that old fashioned car of yours. It doesn't suit your status. I shall choose the model and colour of your new car."

"You are welcome, but at the moment, I have to change one tyre. Bye for now. Take care."

He slid the phone in the pocket of his shirt and tried to take a deep breath. The immediate problem was averted. He was anyway planning an urgent visit to Switzerland for business purposes. He would take her along. That would be fun as well as a diplomatic move. She would be silent for some time now.

"You are really lucky!"

The man almost shouted from a distance standing in the middle of the barren land quite a distance from the shed. Ruthless heat waves were licking his whole body mercilessly. The man was staring into the deep blue sky unblinking and laughing his heart out!

"What?"

He was a bit surprised at this strange comment from a downtrodden garage fellow. How dare the silly buffoon speak like that about his personal matter! Who the hell authorized him to throw a comment like that! What did he think? Just because he had to express his helplessness about not having enough cash at hand at that moment, the man was treating him like his equal! He almost growled in anger. "What made you think that you could talk like that?"

The man did not react as expected but laughed aloud while running around like a small boy randomly across the rough patch of land under the glaring sun.

He watched him confused and once again asked sharply, "And why are you not attending to my work?"

The man replied, "You are lucky...very lucky indeed!"

He chose to reply to the man this time "No...you fool. I am not lucky...there is nothing called luck. I made my fortune and whatever else I have today. I worked for all of these and so I have them at my disposal. I am not lucky. No one is lucky or unlucky and you better get rid of the dirty habit of eavesdropping on other's conversation Do you understand?"

The man seemed to have not paid any heed to what he saidand was now standing bent in front of a shrub with prickles all over. There was no flower but the man seemed to be either inhaling some smell deeply or trying to strike a conversation with the shrub.

He stared at the boy quizzically.

The boy was smiling too and did not care for his quizzical look.

He was now anxious. He could neither run away from there because his car was stranded by the side of the shed with one missing wheel. He waited there totally uncertain of what he should do next. After a while the man came back to the shed in a jovial mood with a strange glowing smile on his impoverished face. His eyes were delirious in some kind of trance but they were not strained as before; as if he had been completely rejuvenated after this queer exercise.

"You are so lucky!" repeated the man.

"Don't talk nonsense. You are mad. What luck are you babbling about for so long?" He asked rudely.

The man pointed at the bench on which the tyre was mounted to draw his attention to the inner surface of the tyre which had been damaged very badly in heat and had thinned out perilously.

"Another ten minutes of drive at that speed and the tyre would have burst. You are so lucky!" the man said with a sigh of relief.

He realized how deadly a disaster he had just averted with threadbare distance. He nodded in agreement. But immediately some other anxiety started raising its ugly head at the back of his mind. He did not have enough cash with him. He asked meekly "Do I have to change the tyre as well?"

The boy responded with a giggle, "Yes of course! Unless you want to commit suicide in another ten minutes!"

He glared at the boy with disgust.

The man casually confirmed, "Yes...you must."

He was now extremely anxious. For one long minute he did not say a word and finally mumbled, "But I have only two hundred rupees in my wallet!"

Now the man also started pondering over the problem.

He asked fearfully "How much would you charge for a tyre?"

"Two and half thousand," said the man hesitantly.

"Don't you have a duplicate scrapped one that can take me home for the day?" he asked.

"No. They are all fresh ones. Not even retreated versions." The man said apologetically.

He was completely at a loss. He asked, "Do you think you can wait for the remaining money for another three hours? After you fit the tyre, I shall quickly go to the ATM in the nearby town and fetch the money."

Now the man was hesitant and with his head down he remained silent without any response.

He was also silent with expectation of a positive response. But after a while he ran out of patience and asked emphatically, "What is it you are conveying? I don't understand. Talk clearly, for heaven's sake. Can you wait or you cannot?"

The man slowly looked up and seemed quite embarrassed at his helplessness, "I am so sorry," he mumbled.

"What do you mean? You can not do the job if I can not pay upfront?" he asked anxiously.

The man hesitantly said, "See…I understand your situation but I can take a risk for hundred…two hundred rupees, but not more. This whole tyre would cost me more than two thousand rupees and I have got this material on credit from a stockist who would come right in the morning to take his money. I can't take a chance. In case of any miss on your part, I shall be in serious trouble."

He lost his composure once again. "What? In case of a miss on my part! You think I shall take away your paltry two thousand rupees! Do you know who I am? My breakfast in the morning cost me two thousand rupees. You think I shall cheat you for a meager two thousand bucks?!!"

The man said in a pleading tone. "Not at all. I am not saying that you will cheat me intentionally. I am just wondering in case something goes wrong and you fail to fetch the money in spite of your best effort...I don't doubt your integrity...please don't be upset."

The boy had gone somewhere a short while ago and just ran back to the shed with a paper pack in his hand. "Eat this," said the boy hurrying to the man. The man checked the content. It was a cucumber sandwich.

"Eat this ... I got it from the food mall for free. You have not eaten anything over past twenty four hours," the boy insisted.

The man indicated that the food should be offered to his upset customer. He waved his hand in dismissal of the idea that he would even touch that kind of food. He was trying to contemplate vainly what he could do to get out of this situation. Suddenly it occurred to him that he might have kept some extra cash in a packet in the dashboard. He quickly rushed to the car and yanked the door open to reach the dash board. He opened the cover and found the packet which felt extremely thin and light for containing that much of cash in it. He checked the content and found that the packet contained only three hundred rupee notes! He became flustered now. This was madness! He knew he had kept some three thousand rupees in the packet and it was reduced to only three notes now. This could have only one explanation. Guessing about what might have gone wrong he became furious and in a fit of extreme anger called his wife from his cell phone.

"Did you take any money from the packet in the dash board?" he asked bitterly.

His wife hesitated to answer for a few seconds and then admitted, "Yes...I did. That day when I took the car to attend the marriage anniversary of my sister I ran short of money for buying the present for them."

"Huh! That's great! You bought a three-thousand-rupee gift for your sister!" he growled over the phone.

"Less than that ... but they also gifted me a diamond ring on our marriage anniversary, you remember?" his wife replied, justifying the act.

"Did I ask them to do that? I can't recall any request of such nature from my end! On top of it when you remove money from wherever you lay your hands on, do you ever bother to think if that money is set aside by me for some valid reason? No ... you don't ...why should you think? It's not you who earns money ... it's me who slogs like a dog from morning to night for every single rupee...you don't have to suffer through the grind..." he blurted out in a fury. The glaring sun was abundantly spraying heat on his skin. He was becoming hysterical with every passing second.

"Just shut up. You have spoken enough. Stop bragging about your money. You have forgotten that you started your business with my box full of jewellery. Without that you were not even worth a beggar on the street." his wife snapped.

"You ungrateful idiot! You have forgotten the loads of necklaces and rings and bangles you have on your body when you go out of the house? All that came from the air...uh? I returned those petty things with interest," he shouted back at her.

His wife was shouting at the same pitch in return, "I don't wish to talk to you anymore. You are abusive." She snapped the line.

He realized that the line was dead but still went on screaming in anger. "Each and everyone in this bloody world is a cheat...Everyone wants...only wants to grab whatever is available...but never bothers to give..."

"Ha..ha..ha!" Suddenly there was a roaring laughter from the man who was once again back to the barren stretch but this time he was staring at him and laughing his heart out.

He looked at him completely perplexed for a along moment and finally enquired in vexation, "What is making you laugh? You think I am a joker?"

"No...not at all. I did not think much about you. In fact I don't think about anyone in particular. You see those stones...I have been seeing them for the past fifteen years right there...those shrubs...they have been staring at me and I at them, off and on, for last ten years but I have never bothered to analyze whether they are good or bad. I am sure neither did they ever try to judge me. Well, we know our existence and we share the heat of the summer and the chill of the winter together. It's a relief you know," said the man with a smiling face. He was breathing hard as if to keep his lungs somehow operational.

He could not grasp what was said but felt extremely irritated. "You know, you talk a lot of nonsense and on top of it you don't have decency...you have been listening to my conversation. You heard me fight over the phone and you were laughing at me. I don't like it. Just for the sake of this tyre I am here on this fateful day, otherwise I don't give a damn to an insignificant person like you."

The man called the boy and asked him to eat the sandwich which the boy was still holding in his hand. The boy asked anxiously why he would not eat. The man waved his head in negation and said that he was just unable to eat. He had no idea of what the reason was.

The man looked at him again and spoke with a smiling face, "You know, I have seen over time, these mountains, the glaring sun, the dry pale grass, the wild storm, the chilling breeze in the winter morning...each of them smiled at me when I smiled, and cried with me when I cried. In fact, they fought with me when I fought. They are my companions in anything I ever wanted to do. That's why...you see...as the summer is becoming too unbearable I smiled at the sky...at the sun... and the sun immediately smiled back. The stone almost burned my skin as I placed my hand on it...I smiled at the stone and the stone smiled back right away and did not impart any pain on me anymore. That's why as I felt that you were very angry today...I decided to smile at you...just to make you smile as the sky did ... or the sun did...but...but ...may be my smile was not decent and so you misunderstood me. It did not work on you. You are angrier now. I am sorry."

He stared at him blankly. Those words sounded like incoherent noise emerging from the mouth of a crazy man. He did not even make an effort to grasp the meaning. The heat was too much. He could not think clearly. He once again felt that money was everything. Just the very absence of money today in his wallet had landed him into this mess and he could not see a way out of this predicament.

The wife

His wife slammed the receiver down in a fury and glared at the floor but saw nothing in specific. "How dare he speak to me in that manner as if I am a thief stealing his hard earned money!" she wondered how he had changed over the years. It was impossible to compare the young man whom she married with the characterless cheat of today. Success had gone to his head. Her eyes fell on the framed picture on the wall. It was taken during the early days after their marriage. He looked childish those days and she was lean and thin. Over a period of time she had lost her youthful glow and had turned pale with a lot of flab deposited around her earlier chiseled features. She felt like pulling down the picture and smashing it against the floor. It looked like a mockery today. She yanked the frame out of the wall and lifted the same in the air but on second thought refrained from destroying the picture.

"Your eyes are beautiful!" she thought sarcastically. "He had said this when we first met before marriage and had not seen them perhaps in past seven years. But I still have them."

She repented at times that she had once helped him survive the battering of misfortune. She could still remember the evening she handed the box of jewellery to him and he blushed with obligation and guilt. He had said that he would never be able to pay back the loan. It was a loan not to be counted in terms of notes. It was his lifeline, the only straw he could clutch to stay afloat from his sinking ship.

Today once more she felt the urge of leaving the household. She looked around and felt that there was nothing really left for her in that house. He had grown way beyond that small box of jewellery. There was nothing left with her that could win him back. She was losing her battle to fate.

The other evening when she was all geared to leave, she knew in her heart of hearts that she would not be able to go away. Though she threatened him that she would take her son with her and leave him totally deserted yet she wondered today, if she really did so, she would probably not take her son with her. She would let him be haunted by the guilt that he was the gainer and she was the loser in the game of give and take. She would miss her pulse but there would be a sadistic satisfaction that he would never be able to pardon himself for what he had gained.

She looked at the watch. There was still some time for the playgroup to break for the day. She pondered over the decision once more. No. She should not allow any more silly weakness to pull her back. There was nothing. All was over. Any reconciliation tomorrow would be in the shape of camouflage. And that camouflage was a flimsy one lasting for a very short span. Once again the ugliness of the true identity of their marital relationship would be exposed in a flash and then the cycle would repeat. She decided not to go through it all over again. Enough has been done already.

She must go. Right away.

She stood in front of the cupboard. Dozens of expensive saris and salwar kurtas were neatly packed and arranged inside the shelves. There was another cupboard which was almost jam-packed with western outfits. There was a time when he used to be obsessed with her physical appearance and would buy all sorts of exotic outfits from different parts of the country. She had never been very comfortable in such dresses and hence they were never really utilized. She did not bother about the other cupboard. Anyway, when she ran her eyes through those clothes today, she felt the pinch in a harder way. They reminded her of a lost world.

She deliberated for a moment on which of the saris she would take. She clumsily pulled out a number of saris those were the cheaper ones and threw them into an open suitcase kept on the floor. As soon as the suitcase was almost filled, she flung the lid on top of it to close the same. In a fit of anger she yanked the suitcase to set it on the floor in upright position. She quickly checked her looks in the mirror and smirked. That's okay for a woman like her. She was a loser and should look like a loser. Setting the suitcase aside against the wall, she proceeded to inform the maid servant that she would be leaving for a while and the servant should go and bring her son as he arrived from the play group. She was about to call her and then the telephone rang. She hesitated for a moment before picking up the receiver because she had some inkling that this might be another frantic call from her husband. She did not feel like facing one more torrent of bristly words. But deep inside her mind she had a faint expectation that he might have called to apologize that he did so many times lately for his ill temper. She took the call.

"So…you must be excited now. Tomorrow is the meeting at the school!" It was her father from one thousand kilometers away.

She quickly adjusted her mood and replied with a jovial voice, "Oh yes! We are all excited. This is a school of international repute."

"It must be very expensive, I guess."

"Hmm…expensive indeed. See…that's how they segregate the

classes. I mean the class of people. It's not possible for a lower middle class family to afford such education. Only children from good background can get admission in these schools."

Her Father sighed, "Huh! Gone are those days when education had no link with money. We learnt because we wanted to learn, not for earning a few pennies. How much was spent for your education in school you have any idea?"

She started laughing, "How much?"

"Just a hundred rupees every four months!"

"Yes, father, but we were only restricted to the morbid text books. I still can recall the stale black and white letters badly printed on pages that used to wear out after one month itself."

"That was because of your careless handling of the books. Don't blame that to the quality of printing or papers."

"Okay…tell me, did we learn horse riding…swimming? No. But in today's modern schools they teach all these things. In fact there is a course of kick boxing and karate even! And that's the reason they charge so much more."

"Oh! I understand. But do they teach reading and writing also?"

"Now you are making fun of me. That's not right. See, the whole school is air conditioned including the buses. Why should they not be expensive?"

"Air-conditioned! Why?"

"Naturally. Otherwise these children, who will some from upper class community, are used to air conditioned homes only. How can they study in a hot and humid dingy class room?"

"I am of the older generation. I don't understand all these things. I feel study is another meditation. One should be oblivious of his or her surrounding while studying. How does hot or cold air matter?"

"Forget it. You will not understand. But that's what is happening today."

"They will interview the parents tomorrow…is it?"

"Yes they will…"

"Why do they need to? If the parents don't qualify, the child fails! They just want their job easy. How does it matter to a teacher if the child is born of a rich father or a poor uneducated one? I am telling you…everyone starts life afresh. Nobody comes with a residual knowledge from his or her parents."

"Perhaps you are right but I like this school. His father also chose this one."

"Is he there at home? Let me talk to him. I have not spoken to him for a long time."

"No, he is on tour and would be back shortly."

"How is his business going?"

"Booming! He is opening a second factory, you know."

"Yes…but ask him to be careful on investment. Now the economy is showing healthy growth but you never know tomorrow."

"Don't worry. I am there with him. He will not go overboard."

"Don't mind my concern because I am always haunted by my own failures…you know well what we all went through."

"How can I forget? I know, father. Don't worry. He is pretty settled now."

"Otherwise how is everything going?"

"Perfectly okay."

She hung up and stood transfixed at the spot stunned. Why did she not tell the truth! She was about to leave him, the suitcase was still standing by the side of the wall. The wild rage was still alive in her head…yet…yet she could not declare that she was leaving…and actually going away.

Now that she realized that the vengeful frenzy was fading out and she was no more capable of doing something outrageous, she settled on the crumpled bed. In fact, she never allowed the maid servant to do the bed. It was her special prerogative and an area of authority but lately she had become extremely unmindful and like today most of the time she simply forgot to spread a fresh clean bed sheet in the morning. He hated a clumsy untidy house and whenever he cribbed about the disorganized state of the house, she scowled back viciously. They ended up fighting over insignificant issues. She found his complaints totally baseless and in return pointed her finger at his disloyalty in commitment. He fell silent and could not argue further. She wanted to fight more but became helpless because there was no reprisal from him beyond that. At times, she realized that she was perhaps making it worse. Instead of trying to assuage the wounds, she was damaging whatever little was left intact. Though she knew that love could not be won by war yet she fought and fought. It was as if a ceaseless process had started without any reign of rationality but only unbridled emotion.

She sat at the corner of the bed and started wondering that if she really wanted to go, where would she go? It was impossible to go back to the house in which she had spent her childhood. Not that she had a bitter or neglected childhood but there were a lot of unspoken painful memories of her growing years. Though her mind never grasped the cause of torment her innocent developing mind had gone through, yet she knew it was not normal. She knew well that every other child did not suffer that kind of uncertainty and subtle humiliation. Her father was a man with a flamboyant streak and expensive taste and a towering ambition often exceeding his abilities. She could still remember her childhood. Her father had business and the time was good. Fortune was smiling at him. Money flowed as if there was no end and he spent it as if there was no tomorrow. She wore the best dresses available in the market; they ate the rarest of rarest fish available during the season and lived in the largest bungalow in the locality. In fact her maternal grandfather once had chosen the handsome young man as his son-in-law because he was expected to turn into a tycoon some day.

But one day when there was a government circular suddenly landed on the table of the young man asking him to close down the factory within next seven days, he could not believe the same. When he realized the stark reality of the black and white type written words, it was too late and the gate of the factory was being mercilessly sealed off by the inspectors.

And then, to his dismay, the whole business came to a halt and instead of flowing in, money started drifting away. But still her father refused to dilute his usual flamboyance and extravagance. Finally, one day, he encountered an almost empty bank balance and hesitantly suggested the possibility of not being able to bear the expenses of raising a child and maintaining a wife. He was trying other avenues of business but they failed one after the other.

One morning she and her mother packed their luggage and moved to her maternal uncle's place. They were welcomed in that house. Her uncle was a rich man. It was a joint family with a large number of inhabitants. It did not matter much financially that they started living there but somewhere deep inside her mind she felt that her right of demanding things ceased overnight. Though she got everything even before asking, yet she knew that it was the generosity that allowed them to live life uninterrupted. She was just a child then, yet, the sudden change was palpable. From then on she started to dream of a dynasty of her own…a home of her own…a family of her own. And that's what she got after marriage. She wondered today, should she leave him, where would she go? She could only go back to her uncle's place. Her father could never roll out another successful venture and hence could actually never bring back his fragmented family together. He still lived alone in a small rented apartment and her mother got used to the routine and spirit of the joint family. The whole household depended on her mother over a period of time as all the younger members left one by one in search of their individual destiny. The joint family was left with only a few members today. Two old men who never found time to marry and their three sisters who fell in the same trap as well. It was only her mother who did marry but lived a life of sacrifice and devotion. The earlier opulence had gone. The ego and style were still flickering like a delicate and vulnerable flame in a gusty wind.

If she went back there, she would have to enter into the same old life. She would be considered a failure like her father. She would live under the generous mercy of her maternal uncle. At this age getting a job was not easy. In addition to that, she never got a chance to see the outer world and hence did not have the confidence to face it. How a professional world would accept a woman of such disposition was not at all known to her.

She was lost in her thoughts when she was brought back by the doorbell ringing sharply. She stood up to see who was at the door. Before she reached, the maid servant opened the door and the boisterous chatter of her son burst into the room. He was accompanied by the lady next door whose child also was expected.

She was surprised to see them, "Did they break early today?"

The lady looked at her confused. "No! In fact the bus came fifteen minutes late. Where are you, my dear! It's already three thirty. They come at around ten minutes past three."

She looked at the watch and felt embarrassed. She missed the clock completely. "Oh! I am so sorry! I just did not see the time. Thanks for bringing him home."

"What have you been busy with so deeply?" the lady asked.

"Just talking to his father…you know he is on tour and is expected to be back any time," she said while wiping her face in a vague attempt to efface any kind of sign of anxiety she was actually going through.

"How many times do you speak to him ... I swear ...when my husband goes to office, he never gives me a call during office hours."

"Huh! It's just a few burning issues that had to be discussed urgently. Tomorrow there is this interview in the school. Both of us have to be there...so..."

"So...you were training him how to speak!"

She smiled. The lady left, leading her son into the room.

She ran after her son who yanked the door of the refrigerator open and was trying to pull out a chocolate bar from a rack.

"You will not eat that now. You had stomach ache last night...forgotten?" she chided.

Her son looked at her with his almond eyes and said in his innovative accent, "Unless this is finished you will not give me a new one!"

She snatched the chocolate bar from his hand and put it back in the fridge.

As the chocolate was gone, he tried another bargain, "Where is my toy gun? Has father got it for me?"

She knew this was one pending demand that his father had promised to buy one toy gun for him but had been forgetting to bring so far. In fact this had been pending for some time now. He generally never missed out a thing about his son but lately that too was happening frequently. Enough of discussion had already taken place on that matter.

She said, "He will bring it today...don't worry...now drink your milk quickly...I will count one...two...three..."

The toddler barely understood the counting but was thrilled with the tension in the pace of uttering the numbers. It made him feel that he was beating some non-existent opponent. Perhaps, that's the innate nature of human beings...just to race...against time...against fate...against an unseen contestant.

Her mobile phone started ringing and she curiously checked the number. She was expecting her husband to come back with an apology but it was not he.

"Is he back?"

"No...not yet. I don't think he will be back soon. I think he is stuck somewhere in the middle of the highway."

"Why? What happened? Traffic?"

"Hmm...no. It's the car. Some trouble with the car."

"What are you doing...busy?"

"You know. I have this silly duty of the household. Busy or not busy...always as usual. But where are you calling from? Office?"

"No. I just came back this morning from a long tour. Today I have taken a day off. Just sitting at home and brooding...I don't feel like cooking. It's been so many years I have been cooking...just for a change."

"Why don't you employ a cook?"

"No...I don't like aliens around me...also cooking gives me some kind of excitement. Some variety in life. It's a creative act."

"Then don't get bored and get onto your cooking."

"Ah...just don't feel like it today. Don't you have any leftovers of your own lunch?"

"That means you want to come?"

"Hmm...you have some leftover...and your culinary skill...whatever..."

"Well...I think I have some good stuff in the kitchen."

"I knew that. Even if you don't have...you will do it now."

"Come ...don't talk too much. Anyway, I have to prepare the dinner. He will be here by the evening, I guess"

She hung up and went to the kitchen with some more vitality than few minutes before. At least, some one would eat what she cooked with a happy mind without a load of irritation painted on the face. Once upon a time her husband used to be a great admirer of her culinary skills. In fact, he would immediately know if the dish was prepared by her or the cook in the house but lately he does his dinner most of the time outside the house. It must be that female who accompanied him. The very occurrence of the thought of that other woman irked her and she suddenly shouted at the maid servant almost for no reason.

This engineering classmate of her husband was a kind of family friend. Her husband and this man passed out from college at the same time and started their career in two different fields. Her husband went through wild troughs and crests in the beginning and now ran his own business but his friend changed his job number of times over past fifteen years in search of better and better prospect. He generally kept traveling across the country for his professional responsibilities. He was actually well aware of every bit of development in her family. Earlier days, her husband used to share the innermost thoughts with him but after the complication in their marital relations took these ugly twists, they were not very open with each other. Her husband tried to keep him at a distance. He, being very close to both of them as well as their child, wanted things to be set right like before. Her husband somehow felt that his friend was on the side of his wife and was not able to empathize with his feelings. So, over the past one year, they drifted apart slightly. Yet, his friend did not snap the link and remained in touch regularly with his concerns.

She also felt a cushion of security in his presence.

The door bell rang and she herself went to open the door indicating the maidservant to carry on with her chores.

"I tried his number. It was busy. I guess he would call back."

"Huh...he is busy...very busy now a days."

"Busy, indeed. You and I don't run a business of that enormity. It's a lot of money and reputation at stake...anyway forget it. So...what's on the stove? I smell something delicious."

"Come on. That's rice on the stove. You find everything I cook delicious. I love to hear your rhapsodies but even if you don't offer those kind words, you will get your lunch."

"That's the point. I love to see you swelling with pride when you are praised."

"Oh! All this sounds almost romantic. Stop it now."

"Why? Your quota of romance is over ... is it?"

"I am thirty eight and you know my romance lately. I almost hate that word."

"Hmm..." He fell silent.

She went into the kitchen to check how far the ingredients we prepared for the main dishes.

From the kitchen she could hear him calling her son.

"Come here...your father sent something for you."

Her son ran towards him curiously. He handed a packet wrapped with dazzling gift paper. Her son tore off the wrapping in excitement and a toy gun was unveiled from inside.

"Ma...Ma...see what my father sent for me!"

She looked at the toy and said nothing. This issue was deliberated so many times in front of her husband's friend and hence he knew that a toy gun was pending for a long time.

Suddenly something occurred to the baby boy and he asked, "Why did father himself not bring it?"

"He is just getting late...and you are impatient. That's why he sent it through uncle."

"When is father coming back?"

"He will be back by evening."

The answer was accepted and henceforth complete attention was diverted to the toy.

She came out of the kitchen and asked surreptitiously, "When did you buy this? And how did you know that he had not bought it already?"

"I bought it on my way to your place today and the answer to the second question is...I know my friend well."

She stared at him with a feeling of gratitude and remained silent.

"Is everything okay today?" he asked.

"Yes; why?"

"No sweet talk with my friend...are you sure?"

"No...not at all. You know I don't fight lately," she said defensively.

"It's a lie. I can see on your face. You are hiding something."

He stared into her eyes with a penetrating clarity.

She looked sideways and for a few moments did not respond. After a long pause a caustic smirk flashed on her face. "You are right. We had a bitter fight today."

He did not ask the details but appeared in distress at this mention and pulled out a cigarette from the packet.

He took a long puff and held it inside for a few seconds, then let the smoke ooze out slowly making wisps in the air.

She changed the subject. "So how was your tour this time? Another godforsaken place, I guess."

"Yes...another arid land...deserted wilderness...but that's my life...I kind of enjoy that."

"What was it? One more commissioning of a new cement plant?"

"Yes...but this was a minor expansion. I was in the guest house and there was not a single household in thirty kilometers radius. Of course, there was the township for the employees and workers but nothing else. You know, unless you see something like this yourself it is difficult to realize how disconnected these places can be. It's another world altogether."

"You don't feel tired of living like that?"

"I am not sure. Earlier, I used to enjoy working day and night on such godforsaken sites. In fact, once I remember spending a full twenty four hours on top of a conveyor. Oh, my god! I had to climb hundred steep steps to ride the top of the metallic frame of the conveyor and once I was there I realized that I had brought my cigarettes but forgotten my lighter! And going down once more meant climbing up once more."

"So...it was good that you smoked less that night."

He smiled and realized that a tall column of ash was already created at the tip of his cigarette.

"Where is my ashtray?"

She placed one ashtray in front of him.

He flicked the ashes and said with mock apology, "I am sorry! The master of the house does not smoke but I come and pollute the air."

She was busy arranging the dining table. "I like the smell of your smoke."

The food was laid on the table by the maid servant and she asked him to come to the table.

He ate slowly and neatly. She liked to watch him eating. He always savored the food with such a glow of satisfaction that she felt that it was worth the effort. He spoke little while eating. Today also was no exception. She always found some kind of contradiction in his disposition. On one hand he appeared to be more than a family man yet missing a family and on the other hand he seemed to be absent all the time though he was physically present. Perhaps that's why the lady never finally tied a knot with him even after having a relation for so many years. He was difficult to read…or there was not much to read in him…a simple man.

Suddenly she asked, "Any news from her?"

He looked up, a bit surprised. "No. I guess she is fine. Perhaps happily married with two kids. She gave up her job and took to the household as a full time profession. I guess there is nothing that can cause news any more for her at the moment."

She smiled and offered a little more rice. She knew he never took that twice. Whatever little was served he would eat only in a single go but would never opt for a second serving.

"Don't you feel as if something is missing in your life?" she asked earnestly.

He did not respond immediately but unmindfully kept tracing his finger around the rim of the glass. After some time, he dragged himself back to the present setting with some effort and said, "You know what…this time I had a strange experience."

"On the site? During your tour?"

"Yes. When I arrived at the spot, the job was half way through and the site was in the middle of construction. The office buildings were not ready but half done. The main central building was under construction and at that time there was only one floor made. The upper floors were not ready yet. So you can imagine the upper floors were all very crude with Iron rods sticking out their rough and stiff heads here and there. The crude concrete columns were standing upright holding the roof on top. Some bags of cement, some broken tiles, some containers made of tin with sharp edges filled with dried paints littered the area. But, due to the openness, there was a free flow of air over there. The daily rated laborers used to work and live there itself. Their complete household was arranged in the middle of that kind of surrounding. One fine morning, I was having a smoke there and you know what?

Suddenly my eyes happened to fall on the railing. They had set up a flimsy structure of bamboo against the wall where they hung their clothes for drying. Among several different items, there was a night gown hanging there. It was very pale and had lost its original colour long back. On close watch, I could find lots of places it was torn and further stitched carelessly due to prolonged usage. It was wavering in the wild gust of wind and clinging to the railing only due to a single clip. Somehow, I had a strange feeling that I never had. The very existence of the nightgown brought an aura of something homely to that barren under-construction floor. As if the single thing fluttering in the air and drying, suggested a hint that there was a woman there…and there were some blushing moments consummating the intimate desires of flesh. I don't know what home is …but it made me feel as if I got a secret unauthorized peek into a home. But that home seemed so seductive to me…I can't explain in words."

She listened attentively and was lost in her own thought after he finished speaking. He washed his hands and lit another cigarette. She asked contemplatively, "Don't you ever come across any woman whom you might want that way?"

He stared at the floor for a long time and then suddenly said looking at her, "You know…I have been tormented by a disapproving urge lately."

She looked at him curiously.

He said, "I want to kiss you."

She did not react but went on clearing the table. After she had taken all the used utensils back to the kitchen, she came back to occupy a chair in front of him. "You never spoke like that before."

He deliberated for a moment and said, "I think I never felt like that before."

He added after a long pause, "I think I have upset the atmosphere and the decade long tranquility. Have I?"

She smiled, "No."

"Well…you don't look happy either. Huh! Life is strange…see…look at yourself…you are burning with frustration and humiliation every second because he is not really with you even if he is back home during some of the nights. On the other hand, he is neither there nor here. I don't know how much he wants that woman…but he has gone too deep into that."

"And you?"

"Well…I started wishing you in my life but then I am a vagabond by nature. It does not matter much."

"Only I don't see any light at the end of it…that's the way it is."

"Why not? Can't there be a correction?" he insisted.

"Correction?" She fell quiet.

They sat silently for a long moment and then she said slowly waving her head, "No. There is no room left. I have gone too far in life. There is no come back anymore."

"Why can't there be! Of course it's possible. It's just the old habits. Shrug them off and everything can be better. There won't be much of a loss. I don't think you love him so much…it's just the inertia."

"Perhaps so! But I can't leave this house like that."

"Hmm…I understand. You know what? We all want a better tomorrow but for things to improve…things got to change. But ironically we never want things to change. There is the trouble. We keep sinking deeper and deeper into a vicious circle."

He stood up with his packet of cigarettes and the lighter in hand. "Now…I think I got to go. I request you not to fight any more today…whatever the reason. If you live this life, try to accommodate yourself into it. I shall call him tonight and perhaps come in the evening tomorrow. For next few days I am in the town."

He was proceeding towards the door when she said, "Wait…you wanted to kiss me."

He turned back.

She approached him and stood near him. For a moment they looked into the depth of each other's eyes and embraced each other. The passionate kiss lingered in their mouth as if for an eternity. Even after that he kept holding her tightly for a long moment and then quietly left the house.

Everything goes...

He decided to give it a shot one last time "Can't I pay through credit card in the petrol pump and they make a cash payment to you?"

The man started smiling again.

"Don't smile like that please. I can't stand it." He was irritated.

"The petrol pump has no relation with me at all. They are unlikely to render such service to you or me. On top of it, I think they operate on cash and no credit card facility is available there." The man gestured at the boy.

The boy asserted by nodding his head.

He wrung his hand in the air in frustration and said, "So, what is it that I can do now?"

The man said nonchalantly without a smile, "I don't know. You see I don't think much. I had little trouble till date in my life and nature solved all of them in due course. I can only suggest that you can stay in my shed as long as you like. We can sleep on the ground and we shall spare the bed for you."

"You are mad. Complete mad! I can go to the town to withdraw pile of cash from the ATM and throw that on your stupid face," he said sneeringly.

"But how will you go there? You can't get a taxi from here," said the man, but on second thought he seemed to have struck an idea and after pondering over the suitability of the same he hesitantly proposed the idea to him, "There is a state transport bus that stops some half a kilometer away from here. You can go there and catch the bus to the town. But can you walk under the sun like this? I again suggest that you stay here in the shed till evening and as the weather softens down a little, you go."

"I am not going to spend a single second in that shabby shack of yours. You don't realize who I am," he said bitterly.

"Why can't you stay? It's your unfounded fear. It's not only me who stays at the shed. In the winter, chill stays with me there, in the summer sun rays trickle down through the crack on the roof and stay the whole day with me. During rain wandering raindrops rush in to my shed and take shelter on my bed. Why can't you stay?" said the man with an air of obviousness.

He snapped, "What do you think? I am a vagabond or something? It's my misfortune that I happened to run out of cash today and hence on my knees for your help. You refused me, thinking that I might run away with your paltry money! Let me tell you that I am running a hundred crore business and I stay in Five Star hotels but not in a shack like that. I have status. Do you know what status is?"

The man smiled again rather involuntarily, "No I don't know. But I can see you are extremely upset about the situation. Your money is gone...your car has broken down..."

He cut him short in a fury, "No. My money is not gone...it's all in the bank and I can purchase all the tyres in the world if I wish...and I have three cars in my garage...do you understand, you fool?"

"I never doubted it...but once again I suggest you stay here till evening. See...if your money is not gone today...it will go tomorrow...or your fleet of cars will become junk some time later.

Everything goes...believe me, literally every thing. It's just a matter of time before they vanish into thin air. You know what? Look there...yes...that open field...you can see a heap of stone and junk there. Ten years back there used to be a robust massive tree...I tell you, you would rarely come across a stronger trunk than that in this area. But, once there was a devastating storm that simply uprooted the massive tree from the ground. After that over the years so many layers of soil got deposited and now it's not to be seen at all! In fact you will not believe...I have seen hard rocks on the hills wearing out over the years...now I can barely find them...totally flattened out. In fact, I can't find some stars in the sky at night that used to be hanging up there when I was a child. So everything goes. In fact once I asked the moon why she came back to me every night. Do you know what she said? She said that she came back to see if I was still there...if my shed was still there...because everything goes. That's why I always ponder as the noon rolls into afternoon, is the moon there still...would she come to greet me tonight also? I know now, why rain, sun and wind come back to me again and again. Just to see if I am still there and I wait for them. You see...I can't hold them tight and they are missing. In fact once I tried indeed. I took that bucket and very carefully tiptoed to that open land and in a swift move brought down the open end of the bucket onto the surface which was flooded with sun light. I thought I had caught sun light for ever in that bucket! But...but to my dismay as soon as I slightly lifted the bucket to see what I possessed...I found it was only darkness...the sunlight was not there! Now I know I can't catch the sun. As I try to do that, it is gone. One day I covered my shed completely with tarpaulin from all sides. I have some extra sheets under the bed. I wanted to enjoy the company of wind by keeping the wind captive. Oh no! Same story repeated. I could not feel his existence at all on my skin. Then as soon as I removed the blockage...the wind started slapping me hard...with a vengeance...I realized that to enjoy his company I must set him free." The man was as if in a trance and was happily describing his experience. He ran out of breath and asked for the plastic bottle to drink some water. The boy handed the bottle to him and he gulped whatever remained in it.

Then with the smile back to his face he started speaking again. "You know ... once there was an old man who came like you to get his punctured tyre repaired and he was being driven by a driver. After the work he left as everyone leaves. Eventually after seven days or so I found him back to my shed again in a desperate mood. I saw from a distance that all his tyres were in good shape but still he was back! He got down and rushed to me asking if I happened to find any photograph here that had probably slipped down from his wallet when he had come for the repair job last time. I was at a complete loss. It's all dusty here and I never noticed anything like that. He confirmed that the photograph was a small one, just a little bigger than the size of the thumb. After speculating about the spot where it might have fallen, we carried out a thorough search and, luckily, we found that the picture was still lying there but in a damaged condition. Many people must have walked over it during the past seven days. He grabbed the photograph and touched the surface affectionately as if he was running his fingers over the person's skin whose picture it was. It was of a small boy. I asked him who he was and the old man replied that it was his son when he was five year old. He always carried his picture in his wallet. He told me that his son left him and lived in some far away country. He could rarely see him these days. I asked the old man if his son still looked like that. The old man laughed at me and exclaimed that his son was a grown-up man nearing late middle age...how could he look the same? He looked very different. You know...as the old man was getting into the car, I saw that the driver was guiding him to the door. I asked if there was any problem. The old man said that he could not see properly for the past two years. His eyes offered him a very blurred vision of everything! Now...you see...the image in the photo once resembled a five-year-old boy who did not exist anymore...or existed somehow as a middle-aged man...and on top of it the viewer had lost his vision ...so he could not see either...in addition to that the photograph was damaged! What is the point in running back hundred kilometers just for a piece of paper of size little bigger than the thumb! It's a futile expectation that the lightning flashing on the sky in a stormy night would freeze for ever in the frame of nature. It never does. It goes...everything goes..."

He could not bear anymore and started walking towards the bus stand. Before leaving he shouted, "I shall be back with the money. Don't even dare to remove any expensive component from my car or I shall come back from hell to kill you. I am coming... Wait till then...or better do the job...keep the car ready."

The journey

He tried to sprint along the burning concrete road but in reality he was barely dragging himself painfully through the scorching heat. After almost half an hour of arduous walk he arrived at the almost empty bus stand which was nothing but an open space slightly elevated from the road surface with one lone cement bench resolutely frozen with the ground staring aloof in unknown direction.

He looked around and found no other human existence in visible range. He could not help but wait for the state transport bus. The last time he waited for a bus was more than a decade ago. Somewhere deep inside his subconscious mind a forgotten memory of his early married life started conflicting with his current state of affairs. He could not afford a taxi then and used to go out during every weekend with his newly married wife. There was a lot of excitement in the air those days although they used to travel by bus and local trains. He refused to acknowledge the fact that he enjoyed those days. Hence a conflicting duality made him even more irritable.

After suffering almost fifteen minutes under the cruel torture of the scorching heat he could see the wavering image of a bus in the shimmering horizon. The state transport buses were meant for the masses and hence they were neither designed nor maintained for any kind of physical comfort of the rider. The sole purpose of the commuters was expected to be the transportation from one point to the other. Generally, they were packed like sardines with human bodies bunched into tight bundles inside the metallic structure mounted on four wheels. This one was no exception and was heavily crowded. Noticing his waving hand the bus came to halt rather diffidently because he appeared too well dressed for riding a bus like that. Somebody unlatched the metallic door from inside and the heavy slab of tin and rusted metal plates swung open dangling outside the body of the bus. He watched for a few seconds completely motionless in sheer confusion about how he could accommodate himself inside this already over packed box of metal. Usually these buses are always in a hurry and a rough impatient voice yelled at him to get on board or get lost. He quickly clutched the rod adjacent to the door and set his foot on the narrow strip of the platform. Somebody quickly pulled the door and it slammed shut behind his back. The bus started its journey along the highway.

He felt insecure as the bus jerked ahead with a loud clank arising out of metal parts hitting each other with savage vengeance. It was normal for regular commuters but for him it seemed as if the whole machine would fall apart at any moment and he would be thrown out on the road burning in heat. The touch of the unsteady metallic door made him extremely uneasy and he tried to push himself towards the centre of the crowd. As he tried to move towards the other side he suddenly found an empty seat in the front row next to the door. Due to a tall person's presence in front of it he had missed the seat when he entered the bus.

He did not waste any more time and quickly occupied the seat. In fact it was a window seat and strangely unoccupied at that time. He reasoned that the hot blast of air gushing through the broken window was the reason for it being unoccupied. He settled himself there and felt himself lucky for the first time during the day.

Sitting there he closed his eyes to calm down his ruffled nerves. A few minutes passed like that and during that period he once felt that the person sitting next to him tried to say something but he ignored it. Tiredness was lurking somewhere in his body and at the slightest chance it captured him. He dozed off almost immediately.

Against the background of his closed eyes, slowly surfaced the image of a young man and he instantly recognized the young man to be himself some twenty years ago.

He was seated in front of a cute young girl in his study room in another place which happened to be his home town. The adjoining living room was bustling with activity where the elders from his and her families had gathered. He was staring at the floor but was fighting a desperate urge to steal a glance at the girl sitting next to him. Finally, he lifted his eyes hesitantly and as soon as he looked at her, he found that she also did the same. They smiled awkwardly.

"I...I think the marriage is fixed," he said flashing a broad smile.

"Hmm...are you happy?" she asked.

"I think so. Why? You don't want to marry me?"

"I don't mind...but we don't yet know each other well."

"Ahh...I shall tell you, I am a graduate engineer with an MBA and..."

She cut him short, "Oh...that you told me in detail the other day when we came to your house for the first time. I don't mean that kind of knowledge."

He was embarrassed. "Then tell me what else do you want to know? My salary?"

"I am not marrying your salary; I am going to marry you."

"Well, in a nutshell I can promise that I am a good person. If you think I am a small executive today...you will see tomorrow. I shall become a very important person one day. I have my ambitions and I shall achieve them."

She smiled and remained silent for a long moment. He said now with a serious expression, "Well, there is one discord between you and me."

She was startled at the mention of the word "discord" and stared at him with her large black eyes wide open questioningly.

He said matter-of-factly, "Yes...there is one. You are from a rich background and I come from almost a lower middle class family. I don't think I have the manners and styles of one from wealthy upbringing."

She waved her head in dismissal. "That's not important. It's the understanding between two people that fuels the success of any relationship."

He promptly said, "And I am in love with you!"

She looked up with a faint smile that carried a trace of sarcasm, "So fast! This is our second meeting."

"Why? You are not in love with me yet?" he asked innocently.

"Ah...don't worry I shall. I met you only once before and liked you outwardly. You don't understand, it requires more interaction before the emotions evolve," she tried to explain.

"Perhaps! I have no experience beforehand."

"What do you mean? Neither do I. This is the perception."

"Well...I put all my attention to the text books till one month back. I just finished my MBA and I had to really slog hard because I did that while on the job already. So, there was barely any time for love. This is the first chance and I got a break...you see...I am lucky...I am in love!" He was smiling stupidly. Both fell silent for a few moments and then he slowly lifted his hand and placed it on hers.

She looked at him with a start, "What are you doing?"

He did not move and mumbled, "Trying to hold your hand."

"When did I ask you to do that?" she asked with mock anger.

"Well...I think I heard something like that. Didn't you say so just now?" he said in a spirit of amusement.

"No. I did not. Why didn't you tell me before that you had a hearing problem?"

"Well…let's not argue on that. Don't we have to hold each other's hand?" He held her hand in his grip firmly.

"Yes…but not now…there's time for that. Now…now leave it right away…they are coming into the room…let go of it," she rebuked trying to pull her hand out forcefully and the bustle from the other room seemed to be coming closer to the door. He did not release her hand still and then there was a furious pinch on his palm. He shrieked and instantly took his hand off.

"You pinched me so hard!"

"Yes. I did. I don't want them to see this kind of offensive gesture."

"But I was holding your hand."

"Yes, you will do that but few months later. Don't be impatient now. Anyway you will have to hold it for the rest of your life."

He looked at her incredulously, "Lifelong guarantee?"

"Yes…of course."

"But our company does not allow more than two years. I shall have to ask for special approval from our managing director."

"You are already approved. I shall be the Managing Director of your home!"

After a few months, the cute girl was moving around in his rented apartment with conviction and ownership. She was his wife.

The vision on his closed eyes shifted few years later.

He was then working for a reputed multinational company, having a beautiful and understanding wife at home and drawing a salary at the end of every month volatile enough to disappear precisely few days before the end of the month. He and his wife blamed the meager paycheck for this disappearance and elders blamed him and his wife for the same. Yet, there was a thrill in that die hard race between resource and demand. Everything was almost normal, till one afternoon. After having his lunch in the canteen he was enjoying his daily share of gossip with his colleagues in the basement and savoring a cigarette.

"How are the sales figures going in your region?"

"Not so good. The market is getting worse every day. I think the boom is gone. Several projects are on hold suddenly."

"And then our competitors. I think we have a problem of quality and price. There is no proper optimization. Look, beyond a certain limit nobody stretches his budget for quality. How much? Ten? Fifteen percent? No more."

"You mean our general price level is high?"

"Yes, of course!"

"Let it be that way, my friend...let it be that way. I never believe in killing the competitors."

"Then what do you believe in...grooming them?"

"Hmm...let's all grow together you know!"

"Everyone does not grow. The space is limited."

"Ah...you are becoming serious. I mean, see, we must not kill our competitors because they are nothing but prospective employers for us. If they are dead...where do we go?"

The bunch of young men broke into a boisterous laughter.

"That's important, what do you say? Now that the company has taken a drive for man power reduction! Who knows who is next?"

The secretary of his department was leaving early that day and she happened to see him in the basement. With an anxious expression, she walked briskly towards him and said with a kind of ambivalence in her tone, "Boss is looking for you. I don't know what, but he wants to see you urgently. I am leaving early and I have kept a note on your table. Right away go and see him in his cabin."

He felt a bit discomfited because 'Boss' was the top man of the business group who had never wanted a meeting with him before. This was the first instant. He quickly climbed the steps and reached his desk where there was a yellow note sticking. The secretary had scrawled the message that he must rush to see the boss.

He immediately proceeded to meet the Boss.

"Please come inside."

The cabin was comprised of imposing wooden wall with two broad windows on one side overlooking the city. Few complex and incomprehensible paintings hung on the other wall. In the middle, resolutely stood a massive desk behind which the boss had his throne. The boss was standing with his face towards the broad window and staring into the horizon solemnly. The HR Manager was also seated in the room. He was gestured to occupy a chair. He sat.

"Look, I think you are aware that the company is passing through a difficult phase and there is an instruction from the board that we must reduce our strength by fifteen percent. That's a very large number looking at our already swelling strength."

He was alarmed at this opening speech but said nothing and anticipated the worst.

"You are one of our good employees, but in such circumstances, we can't help but keep only those who are indispensable for us." Stating up to this, the boss stopped and looked at him with a pensive face. He got the signal and was desperately trying to come to terms with what was just sounded. A cruel death warning. He sat stunned with his ashen face. After a long moment he mumbled incredulously, "I am fired!"

The HR Head said, "No, you are not fired. We give you the option of resigning from your job and we shall write a very good relieving letter. Not only that, we shall go to the extent of recommending you to other prospective employers if you want."

He listened but nothing seemed to penetrate his numbness. He could not believe his own ears...he was really fired!

That was another evening of hopelessness. Whatever little he received as final settlement was coming down every day. No interview call came his way. The companies were on a manpower-reduction spree instead of recruiting new people. He roamed around the city like a mad man the whole day from morning to night but without any luck of striking a decent job.

"I think, we should disclose the reality to our respective families," he told his wife in a tone of resignation. They never disclosed to each other's relatives that he had lost his job. His wife was lost in her thought while running her fingers through his unruffled dry hair. After a long moment she said firmly, "Yes. We shall. But, that should not be like bad news."

He was already in a frustrated mood and remarked sarcastically raising his head from her lap, "No...no...I shall tell them with pride that I have been kicked out of the company like a stray dog...right?"

His wife did not react but said in a calculative manner, "You start your own business"

He sat up and turned around to look at her, "That's absurd. I have no money. Even if I go into a trading business, I shall need some capital and whatever I have in the bank is the last straw, I can't gamble with that money...forget it"

"No. You have. You have good amount of capital with you to start with. I have no experience but how about six lakhs? Isn't that good for starting? I remember, you once said that one dealer of your company started with as small as one and half lakh fund and in few years time he was almost rich," said his wife earnestly.

He stared at her, perplexed. "What are you talking about? Who will give us six lakhs? With that kind of money I can kick off my own business in a small way! You have completely gone out of your mind!"

She smiled and said in a reassuring tone, "I still have my jewellery. It is worth more than that. Please take it and start your own fight against misfortune. I know you will bring back hundred times of that. At that time, give them back to me with interest."

He looked at her in disbelief. Finally, he said, "Are you sure you don't mind doing this?"

"Absolutely! Even if you had not suffered this misfortune, I would have anyway suggested you do this. I know from the beginning that you have this passion for starting your own business. Please do it now. This is the right time. Get up and hit back," she said with conviction.

After one year, one afternoon the bell of the house was ringing incessantly like an adamant faulty machine. His wife rushed to open the door irritably. He stood at the door with a broad smile on his face and as soon as they saw each other he shouted in excitement, "Do you know what I am going to tell you now?"

She was at a loss but started expecting some great news. She stared at him quizzically. He said excitedly, "I have got the rate contract signed. Now, my business will become steady for the next three years in a row. I shall start earning double of what I was earning from my job." He embraced his wife and kissed her passionately.

"Let's go out this evening and purchase a necklace for you."

The necklace was chosen and in the next few months, many more pieces of jewellery— earrings and bangles and other stuff were purchased. Shortly a good fraction of what was lost was gained back.

Only he started becoming busier by every passing day.

"Yes, the result is positive," the doctor said.

"So, you will be a father eight months later," his wife said unable to hold her excitement. He was excited as well. But his mind was excited more by the prospect of winning another large contract than becoming a father. One thing of course made him happy that he proved his potency. Due to these upheavals over the past years, they did not attempt to get a baby and people started wondering if they had any disability. This doubt of others had been eliminated at last. As a whole, he was happy but for what reason exactly he was not sure. Everything in life was sailing in perfect harmony. He became more and more involved in his business. More success he struck, larger hunger he felt for achieving more. One fine morning his wife confronted him when

he was preparing to leave for work.

"Today you must come with me to the doctor."

He was tying the shoelace with his head bent down. He remained silent without any response.

She repeated her remark, "I guess you heard what I said. I shall be waiting for you at home till you come."

He now lifted his head and stood straight. "Can't you manage on your own today. I have some important appointments."

She snapped, "You are always busy! I shall manage on my own. I should not have asked you at all."

He picked up his briefcase and the key of the car. "You will go for a check up every ten days and I have to leave all other engagements of mine for that. You don't understand my problems. I have kept a rented car just for these visits of yours. That's costing a fortune to me but that's not enough. Now I have to always accompany you every time."

"No. You don't have to come home early for that. I shall not go with you even if you are back," she retorted.

He left.

Then, another day after many months, he was sitting with a dozen people in another city one thousand kilometers away. By that time he had opened several offices across the country.

"What you are going to supply is inferior in many respects," said the fat man in the team.

"I have conformed to all your specifications."

"Yes... but that's not enough. All the other bidders are offering additional features."

"Hmm... but..."

"What about services?"

"Services? Well, I think I can compensate you there," he said trying to *judge the flow of the conversation. The telephone on his table started ringing. He looked at it irritably and after a moment's hesitation, picked up the receiver, "I told you not to pass on any call. I am busy." He slammed the receiver down.*

"Yes, we were talking about services. In this product really there should not be a need for after sale service. It's kind of 'use and throw' in nature. But still for your information I have a team of service experts available with me."

"Oh! The multinationals have a stronger team I have no doubt...see, you also will appreciate that they are the legends. Your service team can never be as good as theirs. Their expertise has grown over hundreds of years. Your company itself is not more than six years old. How do you beat them!" said the fat man.

"Well, I shall not argue with you on that. You have some preset ideas in your mind. This argument will lead us nowhere. Rather, I would like to mention that I am a man who believes in profit sharing, you know. Good things taste better when shared..."

Once more the telephone started ringing loudly and this time he let it ring for a while and then grabbed the receiver in a fury, "What are you trying to do? Don't you understand simple human language? Don't try to connect me to anybody on this earth till I finish this meeting." He slammed the receiver and tried to continue with the dialogue.

"Yes...so..." he fumbled for a link.

"You were talking about your idea of profit sharing," the fat man helped him.

"Yes...profit sharing. Let me be very specific. You have already got a price from me, which is twenty percent lower than the others. Hence, you have the choice of placing the order on a higher price anywhere within this twenty percent band. Whatever the difference, I can keep for you all. Once the order is executed, we can all enjoy."

The group remained silent for some time and then the fat man said, "Okay. We can shake hands now. The order will be released by the beginning of the next financial year."

He looked surprised "What? Next financial year! That's still four months away. No..no...I want it right now...say within a week."

"That's impossible. We have many of those items in stock at the moment. We have to first consume those."

"You can sure find a way of consuming them quickly...I want the order now."

"It's not possible."

"Well...you know I can organize some additional services as well...some parties...some beautiful companies...I don't know what you would prefer..."

"Hmm...I shall try to do something...it's tough...but in this case we require the services in advance. Each of us would confirm our preference later. You organize accordingly."

They shook hands and left. He went out with them up to the gate. As he was coming back to his chamber, his eyes happened to rest on the secretary who was trying to pass on the call during his meeting. His blood boiled and he scowled at him, "Why were you doing that in spite of my telling you not to pass on any call?"

He stood up nervously and mumbled, "Madam was desperate to have a talk with you before she went to the operation theatre."

He rushed back home catching the next flight available and finally barged into the nursing home where his wife was admitted.

"I am so sorry. It's a baby boy...so cute! Just like you," he said, sitting next to the bed where his wife was lying, lost in some kind of haze.

She half opened her eyes and fixed her gaze on him for a long moment but said nothing. He pleaded, "I am sorry for what happened. But let's be happy that everything is fine. The doctor said you will be normal within another three four days and after seven days you should be able to go home."

She silently listened to him without any expression and then turned her face to the wall on the other side and closed her eyes.

After that, several years melted away and he was a very wealthy industrialist. His business was growing in leaps and bounds.

"Do you know the seriousness of what you have just said?"

"Yes, Madam. I know what I said and it's all truth. Everyone in the office knows it but nobody will open their mouth because they are scared of him."

"And why are you not afraid and why are you telling me all this?"

"Because, I am in love with her and that's the reason I have been fired today from my job. I don't care anymore."

That evening when he came back home he had to face a violent storm.

"Now I know why you have become so indifferent towards the family," she said spitefully.

"You have started knowing too much lately. She is just a secretary."

"Of course, she is not your wife...just a shade below a wife. You know what we call that kind of females? A whore!"

"Hold your tongue...you are talking too much!"

"I am telling you the truth. She is nothing but a keep for you. Now I know why you have been so disinterested in me for the past two years."

"I am disinterested in you! It's you who is always busy with the child...your only concern in the world has become the baby. Can you compare your today's self with what you used to be five years ago when I was a struggler? You were all for me. You used to be concerned about every little thing about my success and failure. Today, you never ask me whether I have clinched a large contract or lost a huge sum of money...no, you are not concerned about me anymore. In fact when I try to speak about some interesting event of the day, you fall asleep or suddenly get busy with other household activity. I am a human being and I want to share my laughter and tears as well. You have actually taken me for granted."

His wife almost screamed in frustration, "I see…then that's enough justification for being disloyal…enough reason to cheat on me! I know I should leave you and go away from here immediately. You have humiliated me enough. All your office stuff consider me to be a poor creature lucky enough to be the wife of their rich boss. They think I am a failure who could not keep her husband within her spell. I know I should leave you but I cannot do that. You may be shameless and characterless, but I can't expose the farcical nature of our relationship to my parents who still live in a fool's paradise believing that we are happily married. The truth is that there has never been any reality in our relationship. It was all a hoax and nothing else." She grimaced and broke into tears convulsively. He watched unmoved. Then suddenly she fell silent and wiped off her tears from her face. Pulling up a pillow and a bed sheet, she stood up and started to walk out of the room.

"What are you trying to do?"

"I am taking my pillow and a bed sheet," she said coldly.

"Why?" he asked.

"From this day onwards we shall not sleep together."

Someone was pushing him by his shoulder. He blinked his eyes open and tried to grasp the vision in front of him. It was the conductor. He mumbled groggily, "How much?"

The conductor sounded harsh, "Ten Rupees; but you have to first vacate the seat and then pay for the ticket."

He replied irritably in a state of haze, "Why? Does this seat cost more? I shall pay."

The conductor was rude now, "That's my seat. Now get up from there."

He looked at him confused and slowly realized that it was no use arguing with the conductor. He literally struggled to stand up with his straining muscles and finally again somehow adjusted himself in the standing bunch of men and women. The journey did not last long and the bus finally reached the terminus in the small town. As soon as he touched the ground he rushed to find an ATM machine. Right next to the terminus he could find one ATM of the bank where he had his own account. He almost hit the glass door of the booth as he tried to rush into it in a trance when the guard sitting outside stopped him and announced, "This machine is out of order."

"What?"

"Yes…this machine is not working."

"Do you know any other ATM around?"

"There is perhaps another one at the market place."

"And where is that market place? Is it close?"

"Around a kilometer from here."

He turned in frustration and stopped a passing taxi, "I want to go to the market place."

"Sorry…that's too close…I won't go there."

"I shall pay extra"

"How much?"

"Ten rupees more."

"Sorry!"

"Twenty…"

"No…please walk down."

"I'll pay you fifty…now let's go."

The taxi drove him to the market place.

He said "I am looking for an ATM booth."

The driver replied "I think I know where it can be found."

Finally, after about five minutes of drive the taxi stood in front of another ATM. He quickly rushed into the booth and fumbled through the bunch of cards he had in his wallet. Finally he got the debit card of his bank and pushed the card through the ATM slot. This ATM machine also belonged to the same bank where he had his account.

"Excuse me..." The guard opened the glass door slightly and craned his head inside to say, "ATM network of this bank is temporarily out of service till ten tonight. You will not get any money from here now."

He almost cried in frustration "Don't tell me that! I need money so desperately. Is there any other ATM or branch of this bank?"

This guard turned out to be a smart man who confidently waved his head conveying a hopeless negative answer.

"How is that possible ... come on...? This is ridiculous!"

The guard informed him that there was one branch of a bank located somewhere near that place but he did not have an account there.

"Can't I draw cash using my credit cards even..." he enquired in a childish way knowing the answer.

"No sir...the problem is ... both the machines will be down till twelve at night," the guard informed.

He staggered out of the air conditioned booth and stood motionless on the footpath wondering if there was any other way of withdrawing cash. None flashed in the horizon. He could not get his car out of the repair shop unless he had some money. At any rate he would have to wait till twelve at night when the ATM would become operational. But that would be approximately nine hours away and it was becoming more and more unbearable for him to withstand the heat. He could see only one option and that was to stay in a hotel for the night and start for home early morning.

"Do you have any Five-Star hotel in this place?" he asked the young auto rickshaw driver wiping sweat from his glistening forehead. The young man was waiting for a customer and his approaching tall figure induced some excitement.

"Please come. I will take you to the best hotel over here."

He felt so fatigued that without any argument he obeyed the instruction of the young auto rickshaw driver and sat on the hard leather bound seat of the vehicle.

The rickshaw moved in the direction of the only big hotel in the almost obscure town.

On arrival he understood that the hotel was not of five-star category but perhaps the best of the lot in that place.

"I want a suite," he announced at the reservation desk smugly.

"We have only one presidential suite available."

"Please book me for tonight."

"Kindly fill up the following details, Sir"

He gave a flustered look to the lady at the reception and before refusing to put down anything other than his signature he changed his mind. These formalities he could not avoid. Hastily, he scribbled the details in the form with a disgusted expression.

"You will settle with Card or cash, Sir?"

"Card," he commented casually. He would anyway make the payment next morning and by then he would have both.

"Which card do you have?"

Now he was upset "That's none of your business. Tell me which one do you accept?"

The lady informed their preference and he turned to proceed towards the lift collecting the key from the granite desk.

There were two adjoining rooms with lots of space but the furniture was worn out and battered. In many places the polish was rubbed out and the sun mica pealed off. There were cracks on the wall which seemed to have been freshly painted anyway. There was a large sofa set with a front table in one of the rooms and a massive bed in the other along with little other wooden stuff. He flipped all the switches on the wall but only a few responded. The fan started turning and some of the lights flickered to life. Running his critical eye over almost everything in the room, he went near the air conditioner and switched it on; but it did not buzz. He waited for a few seconds and in utter frustration grabbed the telephone and dialed the reception.

"Do I have to tell you that I want an AC room?"

"We have given you an AC room only."

"Come on! I mean a room where the AC is not a showpiece but it works as well!"

"Of course, all our air conditioners work, Sir."

"No. I don't think they do. My room is like a furnace."

"Right now we shall send someone to check this."

He slammed down the receiver. The fan overhead was throwing a hot blast of air all around him. He sat on the bed and waited for the attendant.

In a few minutes the attendant arrived and checked the air conditioner.

"What are you doing there? I can't wait for eternity," he said.

There was no response from the attendant who was by that time staring at the bundle of wires plugged to a panel on the wall.

"Can you speak? I am asking you something," he growled.

The attendant mumbled something incomprehensible.

He ran totally out of patience and once again lifted the receiver and dialed the reception in a fury, "What the hell! Are you trying to fool me?! You send a guy who is doing experiment on my air conditioner! You want money? I shall pay you double the rent ... right now I want an AC room."

"Please calm down, Sir. We are extremely sorry...we shall change the room," the desk clerk said apologetically.

In a few minutes he was shifted to a different room which was dingy but the air-conditioner worked in full spirit.

Once inside, he slammed the boor behind him and went near the AC. He stood right in front of it so that the chilled blast of air could hit his chest directly. To comfort his skin he quickly removed his shirt and stretched himself in front of the blower. All his sweat dried very fast soothing his physical strain. He inhaled the cold air deep inside his lungs to comfort his respiratory system. His unsettled wry nerves were slowly coming to terms with the circumstances. He could now start to think again about what were his options for the rest of the day till he would get back his car. He pondered over it for a while standing in front of the cold blast of air slapping on his bare chest.

Suddenly, he realized that he had complete freedom for the next eight hours. There was no exciting but obsessive woman pestering him for marriage, there was no crying and demanding child around, there was no disgruntled wife grumbling about what was missing in her life. He knew he wanted all of them and he owned every element of trouble and pleasure in life because he wanted each of them. The very thought brought a sarcastic smile on his face. After all, not everyone in this world was wealthy enough to buy such pleasures and troubles. He was one of those survivors who emerged victorious in the race of grit and resolve. He struggled when others gave up and he possessed so much. He had sex, luxury and power. All together it made a heady mix in his brain. A feeling of achievement instilled a sense of completeness in him.

He dialed the reception again and asked, "When will the bar open?"

"It will open at six in the evening. But you can order drinks in your room."

He deliberated for a while about what he should do next and finally made his decision of satisfying himself with food and spirit as much as he desired. His body had starved for four long hours.

The line was transferred to the room service.

"I want one plate chicken lollypop, one chicken tandoori...and by the way, do you have any sea food? Oh it's far from the sea...drop it."

"Sir, we have very good lobsters and crab...would you like to try?"

"Ah! I can't resist though I am not sure of the quality even if you vouch for it. Send one Crab garlic fry and a plate of grilled lobster...by the way, send these one after the other but not all at the same time."

Then he ordered some bear to start with...later he would switch to whisky. He toyed with the idea of reversing the sequence to enjoy a stronger kick but finally decided otherwise. If required he could explore more options later.

Let me smile at the sun!

In the tyre repair shop beside the highway the man was pulling out a plastic packet from under the bed. "Let me finish this work quickly. I think I am feeling sleepy...but isn't it a bit odd! At this hour of the day, I never felt like this before."

The boy replied sitting on the ground near him "Why don't you lie down for some time. He is not going to come for another one or two hours. He has to catch a bus for going there. The bus service is not so good. I saw one leaving a few minutes ago. The next one will not come before another thirty minutes."

He was tearing the plastic packet to pull out a new tube from inside. He kept the tube aside and asked the boy to drag out one new tyre from a pile of old and new tyres stacked in one corner of the shed. The boy brought one tyre down from the heap and rolled it along the surface to the place where he was standing. The tyre was heavy and he started to lift the same for placing it on an elevated platform. Suddenly the tyre slipped from his hand and fell on the ground throwing up dust all around it. The boy looked up surprised but said nothing. He once again lifted the tyre from the ground and this time he could hold it only for a fraction of second and the tyre again slipped out of his hand. The man kept standing a bit longer and then slowly sat on the ground with trembling legs. The boy became nervous and rushed to him. The boy held him by his shoulder and asked anxiously, "Are you all right? No you are not...Look at me...hey...look at me!"

The man lifted his face with an effort and stared at the boy with delirious dreamy eyes "I think I am trying to fight with summer and hence it fought back...I must smile at him."

"Leave that tyre now. Better lie down on the bed till you feel better...now try to stand up ...take my support...come." The boy tried to pull him up.

He somehow managed to rise on his feet and then staggered towards the bed. Once he reached the bed his body almost crashed onto the semi hard surface of the pale worn-out cushion.

The boy looked at him anxiously and said, "Why don't you try to eat something? It's the extreme heat that's taking a toll on your health. They were talking in the food mall that one must not stay empty stomach during this period."

The man tried to smile. "But I am unable to pass anything down my throat. I had run out of food many times before...it did not matter. See that soil over there...that's parched...you can see some cracks also here and there...he is waiting for rain to splash on his shriveled soul...but he does not throw away the sun during these days when it embraces him so dearly. It does not matter...it does not matter...let me talk to the summer...he will keep me all right." The man mumbled in an incomprehensible accent. Only the boy could understand and the boy knew that the sun, the wind, the rocks and the shrubs understood him.

SHE...

She slowly removed the quilt and tried to gather her strength to get up. She had been sleeping for fifteen hours. She thought sardonically, "Death is as elusive as life! The moment one believes that life at last is in a trap, life giggles standing somewhere else and then one discovers that what is trapped apparently is the shadow of life. And life runs away like a mischievous little girl! Same is for death. No invitation is ever acknowledged. The promise is always there but without a commitment."

She had prepared herself so much to welcome death in a ceremonious way but death simply waved its hand from a distance and went away with a promise...some other day some other place.

She sat on the edge of the bed for a long moment and brooded over her life. This journey was becoming more and more aimless with every passing hour. What had she made of herself? Fortune has played a cruel game with her. She reflected on a second thought, perhaps fortune played this with everyone. Only she was not wise enough to play along. She succumbed to the riddle and now she was lost in a whirlwind.

She stared at her fingers which were lazily resting on the soft surface of the pillow. They were extremely delicate and tender, full of feminine sensitivity. She smirked, recalling a comment from someone when she was in her teens, "You will be an artist some day. These are an artist's fingers." She thought sarcastically, the observer must have missed some fine prints! These fingers were rarely used for painting. She idly ran her fingers over her skin. The skin was perfectly smooth with a trace of darkness that is almost mystique. She smiled unmindfully, that complexion could intoxicate the most alert mind. But what happened? What was she today?

She was still feeling nauseous. Her head felt heavy and her eyes were drowsy. She thought that had he seen her at this state with these tired and drowsy pair of eyes he would have mistaken them as dreamy as he had often done. He misread her almost always and she found it to her advantage. With some effort, she rose to her feet and walked towards the mirror. For a few seconds, she watched her own reflection admiringly and then ran her lazy fingers through her disheveled dense dark hair flowing right up to her hips resting shortly on her shoulder. Her slightly broad jaw with a pair of pouting lips offered a hint of wild sexuality to the male eyes. She enjoyed the reflection of her beauty with satisfaction and picked up the comb from the desk. The comb sliced through her hair pulling the strands straight which were slightly curly in nature. She deliberated for a while before removing the little tuft of hair resting on her forehead and then let it remain as it was. As she parted the two bunches of hair to two sides, something occurred to her and she unmindfully looked for something on the racks of the dressing table. The object was not to be found and it turned out to be a bitter reminder of what her real worth was. In frustration and pain her jaws stiffened and brows knitted. Still, she decided not to give up and opened the cap of a lip stick to check the colour tone. As she could lay her hand on a blood red lip stick, a slight glint alighted on her lips. She slowly lifted the lip stick and carefully rubbed the tip along the middle of her head where a narrow strip was already created due to parting of hair by combing. She pulled the red line slightly down right up to the upper edge of her forehead and then stared at the reflection opening her large black eyes widely. "Huh! That's not me! But I could have been that...only for a few slips in life! If that fateful afternoon twenty years ago had not been so misleading and if I had not embraced an illusion like a silly common girl!" She breathed a sigh of resignation. "Life is a one-way traffic...It's written once and never edited again...never...not a single chance!" she thought helplessly.

The feeling of dejection was suddenly so intense that she immediately felt like erasing the red strip with savage vengeance. But it was sticky and started to smudge badly as soon as she rubbed her finger a little. She stopped and moved away from the mirror. The image on the glossy surface was unbearable and looked like a mockery. She felt as if she was one of those extras in a cheap soap opera.

She moved away from the mirror and stood leaning against the window. The window was huge; it extended from one end of the wall to the other and stretched from floor to the roof. After pushing aside all the sliding doors to one side the whole view opened up with the only barrier of a delicately carved metallic railing in between. Due to minimum blockage for air passage, the whole room was flooded with wind. When he was looking for a house for her, she chose this one without a second thought because of this window facing the south. Unlike other flats they had seen in different localities of the city, this one did not have another huge tall building standing upright and erect challenging the superiority right across the lane. Instead, it was located on the edge of the housing complex and there were only few small double-storied bungalows at the foot of the building. The bungalows never aspired to block the view from the nineteenth floor bedroom. The long range of mountains made their appearance off and on from behind the misty clouds. She stared at the mountains and let her mind venture into an aimless journey to the past and future of her life.

Today she leaned against the railing and looked down. It's almost afternoon and men of the families were starting to come back to their nest at the end of the day. One car after the other smoothly drove into the open parking area below the building. From her bed room window she could see her own car nicely parked on the third slot from the right. He bought this for her. In fact it's one of those large sedans in the parking area. Sometimes she felt the pang of guilt when she looked at the car and enjoyed the view from the bed room. Why did she do all this? He was simply paying a price for his carnal desire and the deception he had indulged in. Well, she could release him from the tangle any moment and set him free but did he want that? However, the more important question is whether she wanted what she was getting out of this relationship?

A gentleman of near middle age was lazily walking back with a briefcase in hand. With a relaxed worriless smile he was staring at some window facing the entrance. She saw this man almost every morning and afternoon. Today he was coming home much early. She knew that the man was smiling at his wife who was regularly standing by the window and waiting for him during this time in the afternoon. Exactly as she expected, a small girl of around five years who was playing in the park attached to the courtyard, ran excitedly in his direction. As he noticed the girl approaching him, he quickly put down his briefcase on the ground and waited with open arms. The girl's height reached barely up to his waist and she wrapped her little arms around his legs. He held her by her shoulder and picked her up in his arms. He kissed her on the cheeks and they exchanged some words which seemed to appear very private between them.

From her nineteenth floor window she watched this ritual taking place with infallible regularity almost every evening. This man seemed to be an exception in the building, as he did not drive a car. Perhaps they were living on rent but appeared to be the happiest family among all. There was some kind of bonding between the members of the ily. Even in the morning, while leaving for work, the man would wave his hand to his wife and kid till they remained in his visible range.

This reminded her of her own childhood. She did not feel much about it today but could remember that she loved her father when she was young like that. In fact, if there was any faint pleasantness she could recall, it was during those days when her father used to cuddle her in his lap.

For her, he was a magician who could conjure anything in the world and grant any demand she would make. Much later when life suddenly looked at her with solemn gravity and critical eye, she realized that her father was another man who just loved his only little baby girl but he was not almighty!

She could remember faintly some bits of conversation between her parents. In fact she had not come across another woman as beautiful and charming as her mother was.

"You are spoiling her by giving her all the colour pencils, drawing book and toys even before she has made her demand. She will never appreciate the value of these things if she gets everything so easily, and I don't think we are so rich to bring up our daughter in such opulence," complained her mother one day. She was trying to paint a mango with a red crayon. As she heard this comment about her, she did not raise her eyes from the half drawn red mango but garnered all her attention to the conversation.

Her father smiled indulgently looking at her and said, "I always cribbed for toys and crayons when I was a child. I don't want to see her missing those things...and I think she should try different hobbies so that when she grows up a little she can choose her right path. In fact if she develops a knack for painting, I won't mind at all."

Her mother protested, "Do you have any idea how many pencils she has lost over the past seven days? Seven! One, every day!"

He smiled again.

Her mother added, "An artist! No way! We are not rich people. There is barely any money in the bank. Neither do you care to save a single penny. Who will take care of us tomorrow? In a lower middle class household, we can't harbor the luxury of art or something like that. I am telling you, if she turns out to be good at studies, then she must choose a professional career or else, I myself will look for a suitable bridegroom for her and get her married as soon as she reaches the age of twenty."

She suddenly looked up and said abruptly, "I shall not marry. I shall not leave my father and live in a different house."

Her mother used to take a nap after lunch and during the holidays she would spend the whole afternoon playing with her toys. Sometimes she would play the role of the teacher in her class and speak to the imaginary students for hours. "You...you...why did you miss your homework...come here and I shall give you a tight slap...Come, you naughty girl..."

Her mother would suddenly wake up from her sleep and tiptoe into her room to check if her adorable daughter was talking to herself. One day her mother mentioned this to her father, "You know...she does strange things. She keeps talking to herself! Is it normal? Should we take her to some psychiatrist?"

Her father casually ignored the subject and said, "Don't worry...she is extremely imaginative. It's good, actually. On top of it, in today's world, there are not many chances for the kids to make friends. They tend to become friends of themselves. It's not a bad idea. I am sure it's okay. You never know, she might succeed in future in some creative field. May be an artist or a writer or ... say a scientist."

"Huh! It's useless talking to you. You and your daughter live in your own world. You are always dreaming!"

Then one afternoon, when her father was at work and her mother was sleeping, she sat on her father's writing table with a drawing paper and crayons. She started to sketch a tree and a river. Then there was a bird flying. When the sketch was complete, she compared her creation with what was done by her drawing teacher in school on her rough book. It looked really poor against the professional painting of her teacher which was done the previous day. In fact her mother had not seen that yet.

She tore off the paper on which she did her sketch and started doing the same on a fresh leaf once again. This time, the output was even worse. Again she placed the two pictures side by side and felt miserable that she could not do any decent job. Her father would be frustrated when he comes back home in the evening.

After a number of trials she felt she was failing to produce a good work. The bird looked less than a bird but more like an elephant and the trees appeared too large for the hills she painted in the background. The river looked like a thread with respect to the hills. She felt extremely upset.

In the evening, as soon as she saw her father trudging his tired legs along the concrete foot path near the building, she jumped from the third step of the slip which she was about to climb and rushed to reach her father. He stood there with his happy but tired smile stretching his arms on both sides. As soon as she reached him, like every day, he lifted her to his lap and kissed on her cheeks affectionately.

"I have done something today. You will be so happy to see," she babbled.

Her father looked into her eyes curiously, "Really? What is that?"

"Let's go home fast. You better see. You will be surprised, father," she said excitedly.

He set her down on the ground and they walked towards the staircase in a hurry "I know, anything my beautiful girl does will be great…come" He led her into the lift.

As soon as they entered home, she went to her father's writing table and pulled out a page from below the books.

With the page in hand, she ran to the living room.

"I have done this painting today," she flashed the piece of paper in front of her father.

Her father stared at that totally stunned. "Oh my God! You have a talent. It's incredible! I never knew you were so good at it. It almost looks professional."

Her mother was in the kitchen and overhearing those comments, she came out from there in curiosity. She took the paper from her father's hand and at first she also looked surprised. But she kept looking at the drawing for a long moment with a critical eye.

Her father exclaimed, "You have done a great painting, my child. I am proud of you. See...there is this Sunday edition of the newspaper that we subscribe to. In that, every Sunday, there is a section where they publish one painting of some child. I shall send your painting for that. They will definitely publish this one."

Her mother said nothing but after some time, looked at her father and said, "You get fresh and we can plan about all these things when you have your tea and snacks."

As her father left, her mother looked at her with a grave expression. She trembled in nervousness a little. She remembers that moment even today.

As her parents settled in the living room with tea and snacks she was called to appear before them. She hesitated for some time and did not respond. Her mother called again, now in a slightly rude voice. She stood up from her little chair and diffidently walked into the living room with sullen eyes full of tears.

Her father looked sad and upset. She broke into tears convulsively and only could mumble, "I am sorry father. It will never happen again. I tried so hard but they were all bad...very bad."

Her father could not stand his daughter's pain and he got up from the sofa to lift her in his arms. He made her sit on his lap and wiped off her tears.

"That's okay, for once. But always remember that you must be able to

appreciate what you do. It does not matter what others say about you. Don't you feel ashamed of claiming the credit of making the painting that your teacher did actually? Never do this again. You are demeaning your own identity by doing this. Be proud of yourself. Pride is not against others but for yourself." She understood little but she nodded. Then he tickled her on her flabby belly and she started giggling.

"Now... I want to see a good painting from you... better than what your teacher did... understand?"

She nodded in agreement.

She vowed never to disappoint her father again and poured all her effort into painting. Her mother started complaining about her lack of concentration in studies. One day there was a drawing competition and she prepared for it earnestly.

After seven days, the class teacher announced the result and she stood first. Every one clapped and she was just desperate to go back home and report the news to her father. As soon as the school bus halted at the stop near her residence, she was the first one to jump out of the bus. Waving the certificate in the air with her little chubby hands she ran to her mother and announced that she had done it at last. Her mother was ecstatic but that was not enough. She needed to disclose the good news to her father.

"When is he coming home today? Can't he come back a little early?"

"Oh! Didn't he tell you last night that he has to attend an urgent meeting today? Okay... he was himself not aware of it till late night. You were asleep by then. He is going to be late tonight. He had to go out of town."

Her heart sank. Why did he have to go on this day only? Now she would not sleep at any rate till she shared her success story with him.

That evening was unbearably long. Minutes seemed to be stretched into hours but the bell did not ring. She could not concentrate on her studies. At some point of time, her mother asked her to have dinner but she refused to eat till her father came home. Finally she had her dinner with a broken heart. However, the condition was that she would have her dinner but would not go to sleep till he came back home. At last, there was a telephone call and her mother took the call. She was told that her father got tied up in the meeting and since it was too late he would not be coming back home that night. She almost cried in frustration and in a sad mood she slept on the sofa in the living room. The idea was to meet him in the morning as soon as he entered. In fact, she wanted to open the door and welcome him with the grand news.

She could not welcome him by opening the door for him because her mother carried her to her bed when she was asleep. Instead, it was her father's tender kiss on her forehead in the morning that woke her up and she sat up with a start. After a few blinks, she shrugged off the haze and announced her success story.

It was a memorable day in her life. Her father took a day off from work and celebrated with the family as a reward for her achievement.

The family dreamed a lot about her future. The one thing on which both her parents agreed was that their daughter was very brilliant and talented; with a little careful guidance she could do wonders.

That way, life was going on well. Days slipped into months and years disappeared in a blink. One day she finished her schooling with bright results and entered in the college. By that time they were living in a relatively low end locality where her father purchased a house. It was a colony of lower middle class community. Every family mingled a lot with the others. Sometimes they bothered more about their neighbor's issues in life than their own. Shortly after the men of the homes left for work, the gossip between the housewives used to grow thick. Initially her mother tried to stay aloof from the regular gathering but slowly she also became very much a part of it. In fact it was no more meaningful for her mother to oversee her studies. Hence, other than cooking there was not much that she could do during the day once both her husband and daughter were out to their respective destinations.

She was popular in the college circle. Though she was beautiful and attractive, yet, unlike other girls in the class, she was not very shy and feminine in behavior. When the other girls used to be extremely conscious of their sexual identity, she used to mingle with both sexes alike. There was no hesitation or preoccupation in her mind. As a result, her popularity was immense. As it always happened, men had a general tendency to get misled to the conclusion that the lady was in love. Simple frankness was often mistaken as expression of interest in a romantic sense. Her life was no exception and there was a series of broken hearts among the opposite sex. Still she was popular among all. The popularity started from the very first day when she joined the college and a group of seniors gathered around her with the intension of ragging. She was not nervous and quickly measured the equations among the seniors. The student who was the leader among them stood at one side with a mischievous smile. She quickly measured him from the corner of her eyes.

Some other senior student asked her, "Are you scared?"

She was scared indeed but she said, "Hmm…I think not yet…you people are not that scary!"

"Not at all nervous?"

"Not yet…let's see."

"Tell us three things that you have not done yet in life."

"Ah…well…I have not been scared till date…I have not been nervous till date…and…and I have never killed a senior till date," she said with a plain face.

"I see. What about proposing to a handsome man?"

She seemed to ponder for a few moments and then waved her head in denial.

"Okay…then today you will make your first proposal. Now, propose..." The senior student stood in front of her with a broad smile and the leader of the group was watching the fun standing at one side.

She said after a moment's thought, "Oh...you are so tall, dark and handsome...will you please marry me?"

The senior was totally puzzled "What? Are you blind? You find me dark!"

She said with an innocent expression "But I was not proposing to you. You only told me that I must propose to a man but you look like a boy! What could I do...I proposed to him," she indicated to the leader of the group who was standing at one side. He was swollen with pride at this unexpected acknowledgement of his manliness.

They became friends after that day. In fact, that day itself, he bailed her out of the ragging ritual. There was no confusion because she made it clear at the first opportunity that she was just joking and he did not mind that bit of fun. He shared his experience and notes with her. Every other student in the class initially tried to build some invisible romantic link between them and every other girl envied her friendship with him because he was really charming. But, in the course of time they understood well that there was nothing romantic about their friendship. He used to live in a locality that was not very far from hers. In fact, he often ended up visiting her in her house. But that had a misleading effect. The neighbors started gossiping about her relationship with him. During one of their regular walks between college and home, he said, "I think I need your help."

She looked at him quizzically.

He hesitated for some time and then said without staring into her eyes, "I think I have a soft corner for someone."

She started laughing at his diffident confession and said, "Hope that's not me because my proposal part was over on day one and now what's left is refusal. You know well, how easy I am on that!"

He looked at her slightly irritated. "I am serious. What you find so funny is not always funny for others."

She stopped laughing. "Okay...sorry. Now tell me. I am at your service"

He mentioned one girl in her class who was her close friend, "I want to tell her that I... I..."

"It's simple... go and tell her during the break.... but you know what?"

"What?"

"This 'I... I' actually sounds very stupid and funny. If possible tell her a complete sentence. I don't mind at all."

She could hardly control her smile.

"You have understood it correctly. Actually, I was wondering if you could tell her for me... you are so much closer to each other. But I wasn't sure what you would say," said he.

"Not a bad idea... but I would suggest that you be bold enough to speak your mind. You know women are like massive mountains next to an abyss. Unless you yell, there will be a solid silence. If you shout... there will be a reflection of your voice... the echo. So... never expect the mountain to break the silence and address you; you must address first. And, women like boldness."

"Stop your lecture. Do you think I should tell her myself then?"

"Yes... that's final."

They were known to each other but he could not muster enough courage and confess his love. Few days later, he requested her to hand over a small note to her friend. She agreed to be the messenger.

Her friend read it in front of her and explained that she did not like him at all and any relationship with him was out of question. This time she simply refused to be the messenger of the bad news. She told her to convey the reply personally.

As luck would have it, that very evening she and her friend were going back home in the same bus and as soon as they boarded the bus, they noticed that he was sitting at a window seat alone. The seat next to his was unoccupied. She was hesitant for a moment because he was looking straight at her friend for a flash of recognition. He expected an answer and this was a beautiful occasion when they could have talked to each other during the journey sitting next to each other. She quickly took a seat at the front leaving a choice for her friend to occupy the empty space next to him. But, her friend simply refused to recognize him and went and sat next to her. She understood that he was extremely upset. She really felt for him.

During the whole journey, they never even once mentioned his subject and spoke about all other things in the world. She desperately wanted to look at him but was afraid to do so. It was too embarrassing.

Finally, the bus arrived at her destination, which was his destination, too. They got down from the bus. It was already evening and the dusty darkness almost engulfed the untidy suburb. The smoky light from the lamp post lit only a small space around it. Generally they walked a short distance together before parting in different directions but today he refused to move even after the bus left the stop. He was anyway sweating profusely due to the lengthy bus ride in that humid summer evening and on top of it, insufferable agony made his condition pathetic. He stared at her with burning eyes. Anger and frustration was raging through his mind like wildfire. She did not say anything but looked at him perplexed.

Suddenly he blurted out, "What does she think of me? I am an idiot? I am another cheap joker hankering after her in lust? I am not... Tell her that she has no right to insult me that way. Once...just once she could have extended her courtesy to tell me that she did not want me. But ... but she behaved in such a way as if I never existed...as if I was not even worth responding to. I hate her...tell her that I made a blunder by diluting my dignity for such a silly woman like her!" he started breathing convulsively and finally broke into tears.

She listened and watched him in silence. He sat on a bench next to the bus stop and kept sobbing like a child hiding his face behind his hands. She placed her hand on his ruffled hair and mumbled, "Stop acting like a child. I am with you."

That evening, they went back that distance together in complete silence *and finally parted to take their respective routes.*

They never ever mentioned that evening to each other again; he also did not speak about her friend. The next morning she planned to skip the first class and go to college a little late. As she arrived at the bus stop, she saw him standing.

"You are late as well!" she said.

"No. I have been waiting," he said coldly.

She did not reply but there was a silent understanding that he was waiting for her. As the next bus arrived, they both boarded the bus.

And, that is how it continued for a long time. He would wait for her and they would travel in the same bus together.

The sweltering summer went by and there were rains. The whole town seemed to be enjoying the rains after a long summer. You could see people taking showers here and there. One day some of her neighbors saw her with him under the same umbrella and made a big hue and cry in the colony. She came back home and her mother charged her with a volley of questions.

"Who is he?"

She explained in short because he was already known to her mother. He had come to her residence on a number of occasions before.

"You know him."

"That knowledge does not justify your moving around in this rain with him. It's indecent. Have you lost all your values?"

"Oh...Ma...he is not like that."

"Tell me honestly...what's your relation with him?"

"I don't know..."

"Don't evade an answer...look straight."

"I told you...I don't know for sure."

"What do you mean you don't know?"

"I really mean what I said...may be we are just friends."

"This can't go on. We live in a civilized society and people have seen you two together a number of times. You and your father don't ... but I do face the neighbors every day."

She somehow managed to wriggle out of her mother's grilling that evening but the very question became a nagging thing in her mind. One day on their way to college she asked him, "I want to ask you something. You must give me a rational answer."

He perhaps anticipated the question and said after a little thinking "This is not the right situation to discuss your question. Let's manage some time today and we can talk about it in peace."

"When?"

"May be around four in the afternoon? Can we meet behind the canteen? There is a nice bench by the side of the lake. Even if it rains, the trees are thick enough to offer protection."

"Okay. I'll be there."

At sharp four, she arrived and he was already waiting for her sitting on the bench. His otherwise manly face looked rather nervous and anxious.

"So, you are there," he said awkwardly.

She went and sat on the bench next to him and did not speak for a long moment but stared blankly at the ripples on the greenish water of the pond. It was not raining but the pendulous branches of the tree towered over the water. The leaves were still wet from the downpour that had just happened few minutes before. The crystalline drops of rain were accumulating at the tip of the leaves and when they gathered enough mass to be too heavy to hang on, they would slip from the grip and fall on the pond water throwing ripples all around the otherwise calm surface.

"Who am I for you?" she suddenly asked.

He remained silent as if the answer was so obvious that it did not need to be articulated.

"What is our relationship? It's not me but others who are asking," she emphasized

In a sudden impulse, he turned and grabbed her with his arms. She was too surprised to react but stared at him with her large eyes wide open. He pulled her face near his and inhaled her breath deep inside his lungs. She fell completely speechless and he kissed her with all his pent up passion.

The whole college had a guess about their romantic engagement but was not very sure about it because their behavior never suggested something like that. But after this day all restraints peeled off and they were known to be the future couple. Her bonding with her friend cracked and they drifted away from each other. At some point of time they would almost avoid each other's path. She often wondered why it was so! Her friend never claimed to have the slightest intention of having an affair with him, rather she refused him in the most rude and obstinate manner. Still, when she developed a liaison with him born out of her friend's refusal itself, her friend did not like it. She broke the friendship consciously.

Anyway, it was alright though her parents were not very comfortable. In that lower middle class locality, premarital romance was a taboo. It was a subject of idle gossip that people enjoyed immensely. This subject always inspired the creative spirit of the neighbors and in a short duration the nucleus of the truth gathered enough fantasy around it to make it spicy and worth discussing. Perhaps this stemmed from the fact that most of those people missed romance completely not only during their own time but also during the phase of life they were passing through. Fear of losing whatever little they had, consumed their passion for romancing. Hence, they actually envied the options of the new generation youth. They hated the denials of access to that phase of life. Hence, they always mounted a polemic against such things but in a hushed manner within their closed circles though those hushes used to be loud enough to be heard by everyone else in the vicinity.

"Attention students!" Suddenly there was an announcement in the middle of the exam. The dean of the college entered the class room and said with a

solemn expression. Everyone looked up at the dean surprised still unable to tear off their mind from the paper in front of them.

The dean said that the legendary political leader of the country had just been assassinated by her own guards and the whole country was on a very sensitive juncture. The state government might order a curfew any time. The exam was cancelled and would be conducted again at a date to be decided later.

"Now, I request all of you to leave right away and go straight home. But, please be calm and don't panic. Panicking will not help anyone," concluded the dean.

She quickly gathered her belongings and started calculating the possibilities. Her home was almost thirty kilometers away, passing through a locality mainly populated with people of the community that were likely to be the most vulnerable target of enraged mob. There was the possibility of a violent riot. She nervously picked up the bag and quickly started to proceed towards the exit of the class room.

The whole mass of students started running down the broad steps in a hurry. She also rushed to get out of the college and somehow begin her journey back home. It occurred to her from the very first instance that he would be also traveling in the same direction but in this pandemonium, it was almost impossible to locate him. She decided to first reach the exit gate of the college and then wait for him there. With all probability he also would not leave her behind like that. He might as well be waiting there. As soon as she stepped onto the ground floor lobby, someone caught her hand and pulled her to one side. It was he. They looked at each other with a relief and without wasting any word, started their run for the exit. They arrived at the main road which was crowded with people running helter-skelter in all directions. The general buzz quickly apprised them that the public transport system had stopped functioning. Walking across sixty kilometers was a formidable task to attempt but there was no other option left. So, they started to walk haplessly. As they approached a few blocks, a taxi was passing by.

She pointed out and he almost ran after the taxi which was anyway slowing down due to some reason. On the first request, the driver refused point blank but after their earnest pleading, he agreed to take them up to a certain place which was halfway to their destination.

They quickly jumped inside and the taxi sped off. First fifteen minutes turned out to be eventless but as soon as they started approaching the sensitive area of the town, the picture was changing rapidly. It was no more the anxious running of stray crowd but gangs of fifteen twenty people all armed with swords and knife and shouting slogans in the name of the killed leader running around in demonic fury. They ran in a mindless hunt for any one from the community to which the assassinators belonged. And...the locality had a huge population of them.

She noticed with fear that the man driving the taxi was from the same community and hence they ran a great risk of getting into trouble.

It was a crowded and bustling market area on any other normal day and hence the lanes were rather narrower due to encroachment by the hawkers. The taxi had to slow down. Suddenly a young man of around twenty, scrambled out of the narrow lane between the congested shops. The taxi driver pressed the brake immediately with all the force he could muster. The taxi came to a grinding halt almost throwing them against the windscreen. The young man hit the bonnet of the taxi and at the same time a vengeful mob emerged from the same lane armed with iron rods and knives. In a flash of a moment they were all around the young man hitting him savagely. Spurt of dark red blood splashed all around the windscreen and the gory and violent sight of the brutal murder shocked her to the core. She closed her eyes and clutched him in terror. He was also terrified at that ghastly show of animal instinct. They trembled in fear huddled into one corner of the seat. As the ritual was over the mob turned their attention away from the taxi in search of another victim. They now discovered that the taxi driver was weeping. He being from the same community was almost sure that he would be the next target but in the zest of carrying out this sickly murder the crowd did not notice his existence behind the wheel. The driver turned towards them and said in trembling voice, "You better get down. I shall not go any further."

They could not answer but blankly stared at him completely stupefied.

"Fast!" insisted the driver.

He almost jolted back to consciousness and realized that the advice was sensible. He started to get down and pulled her hand. She was so horrified and scared that her mind had turned numb and was refusing to come out of the trance.

He mumbled, "Come with me... let's get out of here."

She followed him mechanically after several requests and they were then standing on the road. The crowd was still in sight and was running their searching eyes around the place.

Right then, their eyes fell on a taxi and they started to walk towards it. The taxi driver was anxiously waiting for the inevitable. He quickly started the ignition and engaged the gear into reverse. In a swift move, he turned the vehicle and pressed the accelerator.

They, rooted to the ground, saw the huge mob moving towards the taxi and getting closer to it by every passing second. Though there was no reason for the mob to attack them, yet they were frightened so much that they started to run. Without knowing where to hide, they went straight into the narrow lane. Every shop in the market was ruthlessly ransacked and looted. They frantically looked for a shelter to hide themselves from the sight of the violent mob.

"Here!" he almost cried in relief. He could locate a shop whose shutter was half open but there was no one inside. He started fumbling with the shutter and the collapsible shutter moved up slightly. The noise was increasing outside on the main road. But from the wild jeer it was hard to guess if they had caught the taxi or missed it. They managed to lift the shutter up by a foot or so and crawled through the opening below it. As they were inside, he

pulled the shutter down. As soon as the shutter fell down the space inside turned pitch dark. She went totally silent and curled up in one corner. After a short while their eyes became used to the darkness and they could see faint images of things around them. It was a warehouse of clothes. There was no window or other means of ventilation. That's why the place was extremely humid and quite suffocating.

"Are you okay?" he whispered in a trembling voice.

There was no response from her. She was sitting curled up in one corner in stunned silence.

He repeated his question, "Are you okay?"

She murmured something he could not follow and moved closer to her, "I have not understood. Are you all right?"

She tried to speak once more with some clarity, "I am not feeling well. Some water ... " She did not finish the sentence and toppled on the soft base of the cushion that sprawled across the floor.

He panicked once again. What to do? Opening the shutter was too risky though there was no noise drifting into the corridor. He stared at her completely confused for a long moment. In the mean time she was coming back to her senses slowly on her own and blinked a few times. Then she said, "I am okay...only they killed that man in such a brutal way! Do you know if the taxi driver is okay?"

He understood that the horrible incident had shocked her. He said reassuringly, "He will be okay. Don't think of that now. If possible, try to get some sleep. I think it's not very safe to go out of here now.

They fell silent. Like that almost an hour passed. Suddenly again there was a murmur wafting through the corridor from some distance and she shivered in fear. The noise grew louder and multiple footsteps were heard approaching. She started sobbing uncontrollably.

He embraced her and whispered in a stern voice not to make any sound. She was not in control and did not stop. He put his hand on her mouth to muffle the sound of her sobbing. The footsteps lingered for some time next to the collapsible shutter and then seemed to move away towards the exit. At some point of time the corridor again plunged into a deafening silence.

She tried to unleash herself from his embrace but he held her in a tight bond and refused to let her go. She felt uneasy and a disturbing thought suddenly raised its ugly head in her numb mind. She tried to speak but her words were muffled by his mouth on her lips. She tried to muster whatever little strength she had left but it was no match against his enraged passion. Quickly she realized that it was not possible for her to escape from the inevitable. He was tearing her privacy in blinding passion like an animal. She tried to let out her protest but whatever came out from her mouth sounded like a feeble moan. He was unstoppable and she lay there like another piece of cloth on the floor being tormented with mindless lust.

Later she could not remember much about the ordeal but knew that she perhaps went into a kind of coma for a long time. Much later, she could remember him helping her put on her distressed clothes and they were crawling out of the dark pit after lifting the shutter. By that time there was a curfew and the town had suffered a massacre.

As soon as they appeared in the daylight, a military vehicle pulled near them and advised them to get into it. They climbed into the jeep and the military jeep escorted them to their destinations. The complete distance they traveled in silence, he in a confused distracted mind and she in total incredulity of what she went through.

That night she came back home with her dress crumpled and torn here and there. Since it was a day of tremendous anxiety, everyone in the colony was anxious about the other household. As the military jeep drove in and she got down from the vehicle, several window-panes opened in a flash and many pairs of eyes took a note of her disheveled dress and ruffled hair. No one missed his presence inside the vehicle.

The next few days the country was burning in hell fire of hatred, vengeance and brutality. Many cities never witnessed such carnage in their history. All *schools and colleges remained closed for security reasons.*

That night she went home and did not speak to anybody but crashed onto the bed. Her parents had millions of questions to ask. She stared at them blankly and once in a while uttered something incoherent and incomprehensible. Towards the night she developed a fever and felt nauseous. The atmosphere of the house was charged with unspeakable anxiety. A couple of neighbors knocked on the door to enquire about their well being or if they needed anything during this curfew. Her mother almost drove them away in a hurry. Things were anyway getting complicated because there was only one grocery shop that secretly supplied the daily needs of households through the backdoor. Her father somehow managed to organize those daily requisites by going out onto the road with his hands up.

During the night, she went into a haze and started babbling incoherent words unconsciously. Her mother stuck her ear to her mouth and desperately tried to make out the meaning. At last she could guess the meaning and understood that the worst had happened. The conservative world of her parents collapsed like a house of cards. They immersed into a stunned silence. They never ever anticipated such a curse to befall their peaceful existence.

In frustration and anger her father never went to see her and he totally stopped speaking to her even about her recovery. All his dreams about his daughter seemed to have suffered a devastating blow.

After a few days she was taken to a doctor in the locality. Shortly she realized that life had actually taken an ugly twist. Whatever could have gone wrong had gone wrong.

She once more enclosed herself inside her room with doors locked from inside. Pinch of guilt kept gnawing in her conscience from morning to night. The house remained plunged into brooding gloominess. No one spoke to the other. On the other end, the college opened again after almost a week and new dates were announced for the exam. She missed the exam.

One day there was knock on her door and she remained unmoved in her bed for a long time. Then she heard familiar voices of her classmates calling her from outside. They filed into her room in silence. She ran her watchful eyes through the faces. He was not there among them. In fact it was anyway a remote possibility that he would have the courage to visit her at her home. The news spread like wildfire not only in the colony but in the college as well. All her class mates looked at her as if she did not belong to them. Not that she had ever belonged to them. Their faces were solemn and anxious. They remained mum for some time wondering why they had come there at all.

She only opened the dialogue, "How was the exam?"

"It was okay," some one answered.

"The paper was as tough or easy as it was last year?"

They discussed about the paper and the professors for some time but the conversations did not have any life as they used to have earlier. Her charm of cheering others had vanished.

Her mother who used to be especially keen in offering various kinds of palatable snacks to her friends, remained hidden somewhere else in the house. Nobody offered them even a cup of tea. After a while they all stood up and decided to leave. She rose to her feet to lead them up to the gate. Just before leaving, she hesitantly asked, "How is he?"

They turned to look at her in a bit of an embarrassment as if this reference was most unwelcome. One of them looked into her eyes and said, "Of course, you should be able to make out what he would be suffering through. In fact we never understood what really went wrong with you that you refused to come back home with him that day. Was it a hidden affair or some misfortune? Why are you silent about it! Of course he does not feel comfortable with this. He is so upset."

She was crestfallen at this comment. She could not imagine in her wildest nightmare that this could have awaited her round the corner. She fell totally speechless and stared at their faces blankly.

They could not read her mind, but drew their own meaning. "Well…this is not the right time to speak about all this."

They left.

She rushed back to her room, locked it from inside and broke into convulsive tears.

Everyone in the colony got a readymade subject for discussion. The rumours snowballed into wind fantasies with all kinds of dirty spices into them to feed the hunger of idle perverted minds. In a few days time her character was maligned in a ruthless way. Even people who did not know her well started making up stories about her misadventures. Her parents suffered bitterly through those tortuous days. The fact that she missed the final exam of third year graduation had anyway jeopardized her studies along with her character. The house they lived in had been purchased by her father on bank loan which he was paying back through his nose every month. It was not practical to sell the house and go somewhere else. On the other hand, living there would have killed the prospect of her future completely. One fine morning, her mother suggested that she should leave the place and stay with a distant relative in a small town three hundred kilometers away from there. She could finish her graduation from there. They would organize an admission for her in a college over there. This relative of hers was a distant cousin brother who was twenty years older than her. She could never imagine this conclusion written in her destiny. How her father could finally let her go like that! He used to love her so much when she was a child and she used to think her father to be a magician who could conjure up anything in the world in a blink of an eye if that made his little child smile. What happened now? She had not smiled for almost a month and he never asked for once why she did not. Instead of tickling her to bring forth a giggle he was nodding his head in agreement for sending her away from home. Would no one in this world realize that it was a real misfortune in which she had barely any contribution but was a poor victim of fate.

The decision was final and to carry out some formalities, she went to the college for the last time and made sure to meet him for the last time. She never saw his face after that.

She stopped him by blocking his path as he was going from the canteen to the library. He was startled at seeing her in front of him.

"Don't worry. I am not here to blackmail you. I would have done it but fate did not give me a chance. I want to ask you one question."

He did not respond but ran a scary search around him to see if anyone was watching or listening to them speaking. He was silent and waited for her to ask.

"Why did you deny that you were with me that day?"

His head hung low and he could not look into her eyes.

"Do you know I have gone through an abortion?"

He did not answer but kept his head down.

"Do you know I am leaving this college and this city of my birth forever?"

He slowly raised his eyes and mumbled, "I am sorry for whatever I have done. But I am from a very conservative background and my parents and other seniors would not have been able to face the truth. They would have thrown me out of the house. I am sorry…extremely sorry but I could not have confessed my misdeed. I am extremely sorry."

A caustic smirk flashed on her face. "You know what…you are really cheap. I made a colossal mistake. Bye." She turned and left.

After a few days she was leaving her home. A small suitcase was enough for her journey and relocation. Her mother did the packing for her. After a long time her father brought her near him and kissed her on her forehead affectionately. When they almost reached the rickshaw stand, her mother suddenly recalled something and asked them to stop while running back home. After five minutes, her mother came back running with a large packet in hand. She looked curiously.

"That's your teddy bear. I missed this. Take it in hand. I wrapped it with paper. Otherwise it would get dirty on the way," said her mother.

She looked at the packet for a long moment and slowly waved her head in denial and said, "No. I don't need that anymore."

The bus left the starting point. Before hitting the main highway, the bus normally took a long and arduous drive through the city picking up passengers from different spots. She had a novel in her hand but could not concentrate on the subject. Thousands of stray thoughts cluttered her mind. Instead of reading the book she kept staring idly on the road through the window. She knew that the bus would be passing by her college and she wanted to take a last look at the premises where she spent so many cheerful mornings and afternoons. After almost one hour, the bus arrived near her college. There was a small cafeteria outside on the road where she had many cups of coffee with him. Though she hated to look at that yet unmindfully her glance happened to rest on the spot they used to occupy. And…it was then that she saw something. She blinked her eyes once more and fixed her gaze on what she saw as the bus slowed down a little due to traffic. She could not believe her own eyes. He was sitting at the same spot with her friend whose impudent refusal resulted into their affair!

She stared at them for a long moment. She felt like smashing the glass of the window or howl frantically but she did nothing. She knew her heart could not take more but, somehow, this ended a chapter in her life.

The next phase of her life started on a rather brooding and pale note. It was a small town built systematically over a period of time by a famous business house in the country. That cousin brother was an employee of middle management level in the steel factory. He had spent his whole life in that small town. The company built small bungalows for the office staff. The size of the bungalows varied depending on the grade of the employee. Every bungalow had a small garden attached to it. The interior was equipped with the basic facilities but not something that one could call luxury. The rent was infinitesimally small. Her cousin enjoyed a bungalow with three rooms and a hall in the middle. There was a kind of smell always floating in the air that did not allow the inhabitants to forget even for a second that there was a huge factory where red hot molten steel was flowing. Huge chimneys blew clouds of grey smoke in the sky. The town woke up early in the morning almost before the sun rose and went to sleep by evening. It did not mean that the shops were open from early morning but there was a relaxed idyllic spirit in the air. Men came back home during the lunch-break. In fact after a quick lunch, people even enjoyed a short nap. The nature of recreations was also very different from what she was used to earlier. There were very few restaurants. The restaurants offered very limited varieties in their menu.

Once a year the large open fields would buzz with vibrant activity. A number of stalls would emerge on the ground made of large frames of bamboos and sheets of tarpaulin. All this caused great excitement in the rather sleepy town. The occasion was the annual circus combined with a fair. The whole area would glow at night with blinking lights of fluorescent colors...red, yellow, white, green. The conglomerate of stalls would look like a cornucopia. Though the excitement spread into her veins also in the beginning, yet, she quickly realized that she was not interested in anything available there.

The city life left behind on bitter note haunted her mind as a painful nostalgia. Her cousin and his wife had their own daughter who was many years younger than her and they did not share similar thinking. She tried to concentrate on her studies.

Her father sent more money than required to her cousin on regular basis so that they did not feel the burden. The attitude of neighbors towards her was of reverence. In fact her relatives even treated her with care and affection. This attitude made her wonder about the cause. Slowly she realized that the neighbors were under the impression that she came from a very rich and modern background but for what reason exactly she was there was the subject of speculation. Eventually, she felt that there was a difference between the neighbors she had left behind and the new ones. The new neighbors also discussed about what was going on in the next house but they minded their own business generally may be because of lack of ambition or due to a predominant lethargy against competition. They were happier people. Only the inertia was too high against movement. They knew there was another world but somehow found it to be more peaceful spending their whole life in the cozy security of the small town.

As time went by, she started finding that settled calmness stifling. The monotonous routine of the town was tiresome. She felt like running away from there but there was absolutely no way other than enduring what she had. In addition to that, her cousin and his wife were really good to her. They took good care of her. She had no visible reason to complain.

Life took a strange turn one fateful evening. There was a telephone in the house provided by the company. It was only possible to call another internal number in the town but not beyond that. That day, her cousin did not come home for lunch but called home thrice from morning. She could hear his wife speaking in a muffled voice distinctly trying to suppress something. The mood in the house seemed grave. The subtle tension was clearly noticeable in the air. She once asked her what the matter was. But there was no clear response.

Then, her cousin came home earlier than usual. He had a serious look as he went inside one of the rooms along with his wife and locked the door from inside. She felt strangely uncomfortable. She was sure that the discussion was related to her. After a while, they came out opening the door and made her sit with them in the living room. She sat there anxiously. The preamble made her anticipate some very shocking news.

"Listen. There is a bad news. A very bad one. We don't know how to disclose that to you." Her cousin fell silent.

She stared at him in anxiety.

Finally, he spoke again haltingly, "Your parents went somewhere this morning and on their way back the taxi met with a horrible accident and…"

"And?" she asked as if knowing the answer.

"None of the passengers survived."

She was not sure if she wanted to cry. She sat there stunned into silence.

The days after that were full of uncertainty for her. She wanted to go back but did not have enough money with her to book her own ticket. All the money used to be in the custody of her cousin. Her cousin wanted to take charge of her and advised that she remained with them forever. But, in a few days time, there was a drastic change in their behavior. The earlier affection and care suddenly evaporated and was replaced by a strange rudeness and irritation.

One fine morning, her cousin made her sit again ceremoniously and informed in crisp and clear language, "Look, I am not a rich man. In addition to that I have to raise my own child as well. I have to offer her proper education. Now, that your parents are dead, there is no body to bear the heavy expenditures of your studies as well as other things. In fact, the strangest thing is, your father did not even have a life insurance to take care of you in case of his accidental death. The house was on bank loan and the bank people will go for a distress sale of the property. You have actually not a dime. In this situation, I cannot continue paying for your education."

She understood. There was no point in going back because the house itself would be owned by others. Living in that small town and carrying on her studies had to be at the sheer mercy of her cousin. Her graduation was not complete. She had to think of something...some way to stay afloat in that sinking condition. She knew that life had to undergo some drastic changes.

In a few days' time the attitude of her cousin and his wife changed dramatically. She was no more an honored guest in their house but had to compensate for her living by hard work. No one cared if she could get any time for her studies during the day and her cousin bluntly refused to pay her college fees. She became a burden for the household.

One day when she was ironing loads of clothes with her tender hands, she overheard a part of conversation between her cousin and his wife. The only thing she picked up from their conversation was about the neighbor's daughter leaving the town to join an advertising firm far away. Her mind started racing. She burnt a shirt and got a scolding for her negligence.

The very next day, she somehow managed to convince her cousin that she had to visit the college on some pretext.

She spotted the neighbor's daughter near the auditorium.

"Excuse me. I am..."

"I know you. I know the misfortune you suffered."

She tried to force a smile at the mention of the misfortune.

"You know then that I had to discontinue my studies."

"Hmm...that's the worst part."

"I want to come with you!" she blurted out without any preamble.

"With me! But I am going to start working for a company in another city one and half thousand kilometers away from here."

"Yes, I know and that's why I want to come with you."

"But you don't have a job yet."

"You just help me for a few days till I get a job there and then I'll be on my own. I shall not bother you, I promise."

"I am not sure...there are so many issues...I will be staying in a ladies hostel."

"Please get me a corner in the same hostel."

"And...for you to get a job with this incomplete graduation would be very difficult."

"I shall do any kind of job to start with but living here is like dying every day. I just can't survive like this. You help me for once and I shall be obliged to you forever"

"I understand that but what about money? To travel across one thousand five hundred kilometers you would require a train ticket. It will cost not less than three hundred rupees. On top of it, do you think your cousin would allow you this?"

"I will manage. They will be relieved to get rid of me. The possibility of

my going away would be enough inspiration for them to do anything I ask for. My cousin still has some money sent by my father earlier. I shall take it from him. You just help me get the ticket."

"I am not sure. Let me see."

One evening after fifteen days she really found herself boarding a second class compartment of a long distance mail train. She sat silently next to the window watching the neighboring family gathered around their adorable child on the platform. The mother embraced her daughter with teary eyes. She guessed the other ladies in the group to be her aunt and grandmother. Her father came back running with a packet in hand. The packet contained potato chips, chocolates and a large mineral water bottle.

The overall mood was sad. They knew that their child had grown up and she must go away to start her professional life but letting her go was extremely painful for them.

She sat inside and kept an eye on the loads of luggage out of which she had only one small suitcase. Not much that she had anyway. She watched the whole scene with an air of detachment. The melancholy in the teary eyes and the anxious faces around her neighbor's daughter failed to touch her senses in a distinct way. She felt as if she was an alien and not one of them but watching the movement and animated gestures from some faraway island whose only inhabitant was she and no one else. The whistle sounded and the gathering seemed to stir a little. They urged their daughter to board the train.

After a while the train started to pull out of the station with an almost inaudible hum. The faces started to race behind.

Suddenly, she felt like looking back. She stood up in a hurry and scrambled through the randomly sprawled luggage to reach the window on the other side of the bogey. She stuck her face against the cold metallic rods on the window and looked at a pair of desperately searching eyes across the platform. Suddenly an impulse told her that there were somewhere in the jostling crowd, two faces...as anxious and concerned as others...but they were concerned only for her. Those faces were of her parents fifteen years ago when she was a child.

But...she could not see them ...it was too crowded...too alien...too faceless...too nameless! She knew at that instant, she was lost forever.

The warden of the hostel looked at her suspiciously from below her rimless square glasses narrow enough to leave enough gaps between the lower edge of the glasses and the upper surface of the swelling bags below her eyes. The heavyset structure of the lady little above forty always carried an aura of distrust against the whole world. Her every gesture and expression seemed to declare a challenge to the opponent to prove their credentials. She did not speak but patiently waited for her reaction. A long moment passed through pregnant silence and she knew that she was being scrutinized from below the narrow glasses of the spectacles. The warden looked at the fake appointment letter her friend had produced. Finally, she said in clipped accent with an uncertain attitude, "Hmm...I shall allow you a bed in the hostel but there would be a physical verification at your workplace in about twenty days time. If everything is okay...you will be permanent resident till your earning goes beyond the limit. Is it clear?"

She nodded innocently and left the chamber quickly. So...she had twenty days to get a job.

Apart from her friend, there was a lady of mid twenty in the same room with her. They were three women in a room. The rooms were located on one side of the long corridor. The gate of the hostel used to be closed by nine thirty at night. But that was no deterrent for the residents to stick to the time table. The gatekeeper was a considerate man. He helped them come in or go out at odd hours to indulge into nocturnal activities.

One day this other lady took a day off from her work and remained in the house the whole day relaxing on her bed. Suddenly after finishing another pathetic dinner with half boiled rice and stale mix of various kinds of vegetables, the lady asked, "What's your truth?"

"My truth! I don't understand," said she bit nervous internally but tried not to reflect it on her face.

"Yes. Your truth! You have understood what I mean. Even I have a secret. Don't worry…everyone here has one."

She remained silent and wondered about which secret she was asked to disclose. Watching her silence, the lady said, "Well, I don't believe that you have submitted authentic documents to the warden. Half of the time you are in the hostel during the day. What kind of job you are in?"

She now understood the query and she was unsure of disclosing the fact. Observing her discomfort the lady said, "Even I did not submit all true information. I am an MBA and an engineer. Though I just started my career, do you think my salary can be as low as the rules demand?"

"You get more than that?" she asked innocently.

"Of course!" the lady said emphatically.

They broke into a boisterous laughter, and then she spoke to her confidentially, "I am still searching for a job."

The lady listened and said, "Just hurry up. The danger is the physical verification part. They are extremely slow but they do it finally. In case the findings don't match then you will be asked to leave with immediate effect."

"I am actually nervous and this is the seventh day. I am still clueless about how to get an interview call," she confessed.

"That's easy at your level. Just keep responding to the advertisements in the tabloids. You will get plenty of them in this hostel. Don't aim very high. You will sure get a quick result."

She did exactly that and there were indeed a good number of vacancies in the capacity of stenographer, secretary or receptionist.

Some wanted an application but most of them did not bother about it. The employer simply wanted the applicant to walk in at a defined time and date. She did not want to leave a single stone unturned. She started to appear for as many interviews as possible.

"Describe your academic background?"

She described the truth...an incomplete graduation.

"I see...so you are not a graduate. Where did you work before?"

She replied, "Never before."

"Hmm...what's your typing speed?"

"I have no idea. I have never typed before."

"I am sure you've never heard about shorthand...have you?"

"No"

"No point asking but any familiarity with computers?"

"Not really."

"I am confused why you are here. You can leave."

"Should I wait for the decision?"

"No."

The conversation repeated number of times successively. She had no answer. The days were vanishing fast. The deadline was getting nearer by every miserable failure. She could barely sleep in anxiety. Going back to her cousin was a bad idea. If they threw her out of the hostel, she did not know where to go next. She knew she could not afford to give up but could not see a way out either.

That night she just could not keep her eyes closed for a few seconds in a row and finally after midnight she decided to get up and take a walk in the compound. It was impossible to sleep. She quietly walked out of the corridor and arrived at the open space in front of the building. The main entrance was closed. It was a large iron gate with an alert guard watching at night. As she was walking lazily in the compound, suddenly there was a sound from the entrance side. She turned. There was a thin crack between the edge of the Iron Gate and the wall. Someone was pushing the gate stealthily from outside. Slowly the gate opened wide enough to let one person pass through the crack. One of the girls staying in the hostel tiptoed into the compound.

She stared at her with a stunned look. As their eyes met, the girl flashed an awkward smile. She saw the girl going towards the corridor without making any sound of her footsteps. She followed the girl for almost no reason but lame curiosity. As she almost caught her, she asked "What kind of job do you do…this is past midnight!"

The girl quickly opened the door of her room and pulled her inside. The room was dark with other two residents lost in their slumber.

The girl did not switch on the light because the warden could see the flash of light. They sat on an empty bed and the girl answered her question, "I don't do any job really."

She was confused. "That means you are also looking for a break like me!"

"No…I don't look for any more. I sell something and that pays me off well. Only this entrance is the problem. But the watchman can be purchased easily."

"What do you sell?"

"My beauty…see…it's still growing in leaps and bounds every day."

"How did you manage the verification part?"

"The man who does the check is obliged to me."

"It's all bizarre!"

"Huh…I am not afraid of anybody here…only that warden…that ugly old thing. Even she can't throw me out. Her husband needs me. Hence, you just try to forget what you saw tonight. In case you gossip, it does not matter because you know who all want me here. I am not scared."

"I don't like to gossip for nothing. But, can you tell me if there is any girl here who works as a receptionist or a stenographer?"

"Of course there is. Can you see her there? That lady is working for a private firm as a secretary."

"Would you introduce me to her?"

"Not now!"

"I mean tomorrow."

"Hmm…no problem. Only her timing is very odd. She goes to work in the morning and comes back at night."

"That's not odd!"

"Well…I generally sleep during the day and work at night."

Next day she gathered some information about typing speed and shorthand. But it was clear to her that those things required prolonged practice to learn. Still when she looked at the calendar, she shivered in anxiety. Only few days were left for the verification to be done and the fake address would be disclosed. As she stared from her window at the vibrant world, it looked like a hostile animal lurking beyond the fence to pounce on her. She made up her mind that she would say whatever the interviewer wanted to hear.

"What is your speed in typing?"

"Sixty-five words per minute"

"Oh! That's very good"

"Shorthand?"

"I know."

"You are familiar with computers?"

"Hmm…I know Microsoft Office, Power point and Excel"

"Any prior experience?"

"No…but I have to start somewhere."

"You are smart. The only downside is your lack of experience. That's manageable. Okay…to be sure, I would request you to sit for this real life test if you don't mind.

Blood rushed out of her face. She sat unmoved without offering a nod of consent. The man dictated and she fumbled on the key board blindly. Quickly her bluff was detected.

"It's a pity. You have been lying. Please leave right now."

She staggered out of the place mortified. It was shameful. She felt like killing herself.

Few more interviews went with similar consequences and one fine morning the warden called her.

"Listen...you can inform your employer that there will be a physical check and one of our employees will visit your workplace for verification."

Her jaws hung haplessly. Her days were over. She silently nodded and went out of the chamber. There was another interview scheduled in the morning. She put on her most beautiful dress, applied a little make up on her face. The lipstick and creams were borrowed from her friend the previous evening. She checked her image in the broken mirror in the room. There was something eerie that made her slightly uneasy. The dress was not so decent and exposed her voluptuous curves arrogantly. May be this would work. She finally left for the interview.

"So you have no experience!" The man seemed to be the owner of the company and was taking the interview personally.

"No...but I can learn anything quickly. Just one chance I need." She was almost on her knees. No effort could hide her desperation for the job.

"You say that you are conversant with computers."

"Yes...I am." She waited anxiously.

"Your speed in typing?"

"Sixty-five."

"And you know short hand as well. What's your speed in that?"

She missed this information and remained silent for a few moments and blindly said "Thirty."

He glanced at her without any expression.

"Who all are there in your family?"

"Nobody."

"You are not married yet, I guess."

"No."

"Hmm..." he stared at her intently. His penetrating eyes surveyed every inch of her physical existence. She felt uncomfortable and twitched on her chair while looking sideways. After a long moment of speechless observation, suddenly he said "You can join us from tomorrow. You will be my secretary."

He called another man on the intercom and told him to hand over the appointment letter immediately. She could not control her excitement; as if some crushing burden was suddenly lifted from above her crumbled head. She would not be thrown out of the hostel. She could fight back her misfortune. She almost trembled with an overwhelming emotion.

As she was leaving the reception area there were several other candidates waiting for their turn of interview. The receptionist seemed to be speaking to the boss.

"Sir, there are many other candidates waiting for their turn since the morning...okay...okay...fine, sir. I shall ask them to go back...okay. Thank you, sir."

She arrived at the hostel and rushed to the warden's room. The angry woman of late middle age was placing her stringent instruction about the verification to be carried out. She barged into the chamber and announced that she had resigned from her earlier job and joined a new one just an hour back. She flashed the appointment letter.

The following morning she was extremely excited about the new frontier ahead of her. She arrived on time and was called to attend the boss immediately. Immediately a lot of responsibilities were bestowed on her. She wanted to do every job as best as she could but the biggest trouble she faced was in taking notes. She had done that during her college days but it was not the same thing. She was extremely slow and frequently missed out what was narrated. Because of the anxiety that her misinformation during the interview might be quickly found out by the boss, she could not dare to ask for a repetition. She tried to apply her own judgment and fill the void while trying to type the same on the computer. She was anyway taking some lesson from the woman who lived in her hostel about how to type. Hence, the basic knowledge was there already. Only the whole process took a very long time always.

There was something uncanny in the whole affair. The owner of the company, a middle aged man of impressive disposition, never even for once raised his eye brow about her inefficiency.

It was all fine and she was slowly learning to take dictation and handle the key board with greater degree of swiftness.

Another thing that she did not miss was that a pair of roving eyes always trailed behind her whenever she entered the boss's cabin. In the beginning, she often felt uneasy in front of the man but slowly it became a way of life that she would be looked at in a brazen way. The stare would not leave an inch of her body. She tried to completely ignore that eerie look because there was no other option she could think of.

One afternoon when she was all prepared to leave for the day, the boss called her inside his cabin and asked her to stay back. The request was so abrupt and unexpected that she could not deliberate on the decision whether she should agree or not. After about half an hour when the office was almost empty she was asked to come inside the boss's chamber once more. She went.

"You bluffed!" The man looked straight into her eyes.

She was anyway nervous and was anticipating what was about to happen. Those two words caught her completely off guard.

She could not respond immediately and only looked at him blankly.

"You should not be surprised that I know you bluffed."

Again a silence and by then she knew that the end was coming very fast.

"You have never typed before...you have never worked with a computer...and you claimed your speed in typing was sixty-five!"

Now she was ashamed and felt like running away from there in distress.

"Ah...shorthand! That's another thing. You said you knew shorthand."

The man rose to his feet and walked up to the broad window. No one said anything. He stared at the scene on the road below his cabin. She sat in her chair with her head down.

Without turning he said in calm voice, "I need a secretary who can really assist me in my work. What do you think I should do with you?"

She was completely broken. She slowly lifted her face and tried to look at him. In a state of despondence, she pleaded, "Please bear with me for a few more days and I shall show better performance. I have nowhere to go. They will not even allow me to stay in the hostel. I will be on the road if you fire me."

He started laughing.

She was startled and looked at him confused and nervous.

"But what do I get for not firing you, apart from a host of wrongly drafted letters and badly noted dictation?"

"I will improve."

"You will, of course, because I shall send you for professional training to master these skills. But I think I should be a little considerate for a beautiful lady like you whose beauty can perhaps compensate for her inefficiency."

She dropped her eyes to the ground at her feet. She now realized what he was trying to indicate. She blushed with shame at that indecent proposal but knew for sure that she could not help but accept the deal. There was nothing to bargain for decency. She remained silent.

"Did you think I believed you when you said that your speed in short hand was thirty and your speed in typing was sixty-five!"

She did not respond.

"Right at that moment I knew that you were lying. But then there were other things you could offer. So? Is the deal on?" He was staring with that penetrating roving eye at her. She felt the stare was burning like hellfire and she was about to turn into ashes.

After a long silence he concluded, "Okay…I take your silence as your consent."

That night when she was coming back to her hostel with a tired and denigrated soul, the sickening memory of the day when the riot had broken in the city ten years back slowly surfaced in her mind. The only difference was that those days she had found life to be grossly unjust for her and these days she knew that life had taken her for granted. She could only submit to the vagaries of fate but not strike back.

"You are not a virgin but as tender and delicate as one." He ran his fingers over her soft dusky skin. She was lying on the bed with her legs curled and knees close to her chest. Her hands were in a vain gesture to protect her modesty which was already plundered by him. She hated every moment of it and tried to get through the ordeal with as much detachment as possible but finally when all was over she felt sick about something. She despised the reality that she enjoyed the pain and humiliation in some way. She never uttered a single word during the whole evening but kept struggling with her conscience. Now this dilemma and guilt tormented her with ruthless ferocity.

He behaved as if he had never slept with a woman in decades and almost tore off her clothes as soon as he got her at his disposal.

She scrambled on the ground for her clothes in the dimly lit room and finally picked them up. As she saw them closely, she almost cried in frustration, "These are torn…I have only few of these."

He turned and looked at her with a faint smile. "Buy a dozen tomorrow and send the bill to me. I think I want to kiss you once more."

She went for training and honed the requisite skills at a very fast pace. The intellectual base was there more than necessary and over time she turned out to be almost indispensable for his daily affairs. Even for business decisions, he started taking her opinions. But at the back of her mind, she knew well that she was being transformed into another identity that she had not intended to be. The inmates in the hostel began considering her to be one of those few independent and responsible women with inherent strength. She never disclosed to anyone the price she paid for her existence. She decided not to look at the dark pit in her life that was growing into a crevasse with every passing day.

It was another fateful evening and she faked several orgasms. He was lying next to her with a mixed expression on his face. He was looking at her with a faint chuckle. She could read him well by then. She knew he was overflowing with a feeling of achievement. He was thinking that he had the power of driving her passion to the peak. He was convinced that the pleasure was shared and consensual. He might have even harbored in his mind an impression that she was kind of obliged to him for that favour.

She said plaintively, "I am sorry!"

He was startled. "For what?"

She gathered the crumpled bed sheet and sat up on the bed wrapping the cloth around her chest. "I don't feel like leaving you but I have to go."

He was puzzled. "I don't understand. We shall meet again tomorrow morning."

"No. We shall not. I am quitting this job. I can't ask for a salary hike from you. I feel guilty that I have been using your feeling for me. I must go. I've got another job."

"It's impossible. You are not going away. How much are you going to get?"

She did not respond but buried her face on his hairy chest and after a long moment murmured. "Our relationship was priceless and I can't fix a price for that. I'd rather go."

He held her face up and said firmly, "You will not go anywhere. I will make your compensation double from this month."

That night as she was lying on her bed in the hostel an unconscious smirk flickered on her delicate lips. She thought sardonically, "So... this time who is the victim? Not me... I have nothing to lose. I cannot lose the game anymore because I have already lost whatever I had. I can only gain!"

Once she fell sick and could not attend office for seven days. As she was lying lazily on her bed in the hostel, someone told her that there was a very handsome guest waiting for her at the reception. She quickly went there and found him waiting at the reception with an anxious face.

"Is it serious?"

"No...I am almost okay. Why did you take the trouble of coming here? I would have joined office on Monday."

"I was nervous. I thought you had left me!"

She noted the comment and stored it in some corner of her mind to use it later.

"How do you live here? It's a shabby place to put up in. Let's go out and have a cup of coffee. I think I should do something. Get ready fast. I can't even sit here for long. It's dingy and almost suffocating. I need fresh air. Why can't they install an air conditioner in the lobby? I want to come to your room."

She flashed an amused chuckle. "They won't allow. This is not your office."

He sipped his thick dark coffee from a small cup. "I'll arrange a better place for you in the heart of the city. How can you stay here! It's so dull and lifeless out here."

She was observing him. "I am a petty secretary who can afford either a rent or a square meal...not both."

He snapped, "Don't say that. I don't like to hear such misery from that beautiful mouth that I would love to kiss a thousand times a day."

"How does it matter? I stay at a dingy ladies hostel or in a posh private apartment, this mouth remains at your disposal anyway. You bought it long back."

"Did I buy that? You could say that!" He was upset and turned his gaze in another direction.

She inspected his pensive face and held his chin with her delicate fingers to turn in her direction. "I never said I sold but I said you bought. Who am I? I can't even dare to say that I love you...can I?"

He was electrified at this statement. "Did you say that? Please say that again...please."

"I can't say that I love you...can I?"

"You can ... and please say so."

"Huh...what happens to your wife?"

He fell silent. The sound of the metallic spoon knocking the porcelain cup filled the air. While stirring the coffee unmindfully he mumbled, "Our marriage is like a zombie. It died long back."

"Hmm...But she is still there and you have a kid as well."

He looked at her with an expression of helplessness.

Later during the day she reflected on the whole conversation many a times and found his expression somewhere in the middle of being funny and disgusting.

However, she said, "And you want me to confess that I love you! Can you yourself do that?"

"I fell for you the very first day you came for the interview."

Life went on. One fine day a scandal erupted. It was not so much of a scandal but his hasty action resulted into a disastrous outcome. He fired one young employee on account of harassing the secretary of the boss. She was that secretary in the middle of this fiasco. It was a fact that the young man had a crush on her and often made it evident in his gesture towards her. She ignored the whole affair. Though the nocturnal relation she shared with the owner of the company was an open secret yet, no one dared to talk about it in public. As it always happened in professional world, there was politics among the people. The young man was a blue eyed boy of the owner and there was a rival group. Someone reported to the boss about the young man's romantic inclination towards his secretary and he himself realized one day that the information was not totally baseless. And…it was then that he lost his rationality and straightaway sacked him without even an hour's notice. The young man went to meet his wife in a fit of anger and vengeance to describe his boss's peccadilloes.

That evening, she received a frantic call from his wife, "You are a bitch! Why are you after my family? What on earth have I done to you?"

She half expected such a response but did not know how it would sound or feel when it came. She remained silent, holding the receiver next to her ear.

In a fit of anger, his wife went on, "Why can't you find someone else? Why? Why do you want to destroy the lives of my child and me? Can't you understand that you are nothing but a keep for him?"

She did not respond. The words poured into her brain like hot molten lava. She wanted to retort back with vengeance but strangely found the allegation to be not completely baseless. There was a kernel of truth in it and his wife was bluntly pointing her finger at that.

The voice screamed from the other end, "You are not replying to me! How could you? You know what you are doing but that's your profession. Nothing new for you! Who knows how many households you have ruined in the past…and now it's my turn…let me warn you…you don't know me yet. I…I…"

She slowly put down the receiver and pulled the wire out to stop any more calls. She sat on the sofa and started thinking about what was said. The more she thought about it, she felt that there was no single face of reality. Reality was like a mirror. Everyone saw something different in it. What she said about her was not untrue but at the same time, she knew it was not the fact either. But…but above all that, what haunted her time and again were the words: "Don't you understand that you are nothing but a keep for him?"

She was terribly upset and kept awake the whole night. In the morning when she had just dozed off from sheer fatigue, she was awakened by a vicious thud on the door. She blinked her haze away and scrambled to open the door.

"Why are you not taking my call?" He pushed her to one side and entered the room.

"Oh! I just fell asleep in the morning," she said groggily.

"Hmm...look...don't make me anxious like this again. I should not have come like this. You know what happened? I made innumerable calls to you without any response. I became anxious and rushed to see you."

"I shall just get ready and come to office. Wait for ten minutes," she said in a hurry.

"It's okay. Take your time and come. I'll go now. It's not very prudent, at the moment, to travel together. You take a taxi and come."

She did that.

After that few days were very formal. They did not meet outside their workplace and the tension in the office was palpable. He appeared extremely serious and solemn. His employees preferred to stay away from him. She did not know if she should feel relieved or upset. She started to get confused about what she wanted from life.

One fine afternoon, she was taking dictation from him like any other day, "We can grant you another three percent discount provided you accept a credit period of..." he suddenly stopped in the middle of the sentence!

She looked up "Yes? Then?"

He stared at her intently and said, "How long? It's madness. Am I a sissy boy that I shall be afraid of her and refrain from living my life?"

She could not understand "What do you mean by that? I guess it's not part of the letter!"

He did not care to explain the sudden diversion. "I said how many more days shall I not see you? Now it's gone beyond my tolerance. I want you badly and why not? That idiot says that she hates sleeping with me. She thinks I am dying to lay her! Come on...it used to be almost like rape when

I had to invoke my physical urge to have sex with her. She is stale like an inanimate object and she thinks I can't live without screwing her!"

She stared at him vaguely without any expression. He rose to his feet and came round the large desk. She turned her head to maintain an eye contact with him. He stood in front of her breathing heavily, "I can't live like this. I want to hold you ... I want to smell your breath ... I want to kiss you...right now!"

She stiffened and turned pale in a kind of fearful presentiment. There was a demonic glint in his eyes. She tried to push her chair back and stand up. He suddenly grabbed her and fixed his lips on hers with savage ferocity.

And...it was then that the door of the cabin flung open. His wife was standing at the door with her eyes glaring like hell fire. She stood there rooted like a statue but said nothing. After a long moment she turned and left, slamming the door behind her.

In a few minutes, he gathered his belongings and rushed out of the office.

Next few days he did not appear in the office. Nobody had a clue about him. The way his wife had left the office that day right from the door of his cabin, everyone had their wildest imaginations running but no one did the blunder of discussing the subject openly. She kept attending her work without any interruption. She had no other way than to come to office and look forward to his arrival because he was not reachable through any means of communication after that day. She was becoming more and more anxious with every passing day. She herself tried to understand the cause of her anxiety but whenever the probable reason flashed in her mind, she turned her face from it.

One day, he arrived in office and behaved perfectly professional throughout the day. Finally in the afternoon, he told her while signing few papers, "Let's meet this afternoon and discuss few things." She nodded. She expected herself to be upset with another meeting but to her surprise and dismay she realized that she was happy; as if she was eagerly waiting for that meeting.

"Look…she wanted to leave me."

"Meaning?"

"She wanted to divorce me."

"I see; and your son?"

"She wanted to take him with her"

"And what did you do?"

"I could not let her go. I can not lose my son."

"So…how is it that she did not leave you and is still your wife?"

"I gave my word that I would not keep any relation with you in future."

"I see. So, that's what you wanted to tell me after office hours?"

"Yes…I mean no. I just wanted to let you know."

"So, are you coming tonight to my apartment?"

He remained silent.

"I am asking you something. Are you coming to my apartment with me now or not?"

He slowly waved his head in denial but did not look at her.

"Oh! I have understood now. You are another one like so many. From the beginning I knew that you will dump me one day because your bloody wife will hector you into doing that. Go…go back like a baby to your wife's lap and cuddle like a meek animal…go!" She stood up and was ready to leave. He held her hand in a reflex and pleaded, "Please stay."

She looked at him and said in a stern voice, "You will get the key of your room tomorrow morning along with my resignation letter. Good bye!" She pulled her hand forcibly.

He held it tightly.

"You are hurting me. Leave right now. I want to go."

He stood up and looked at her pensively, "Let's go and spend the evening but please try to understand my situation. I can't stay at night at your place."

They traveled in his car in silence. That evening she turned mindlessly passionate. The unforeseen animal desire took him totally off guard and he was swept away by her blinding passion. At the end he left her place totally spent and exhausted. As his car disappeared from the parking lot, she broke into a wild laughter that turned into convulsive tears at the end.

During the next few days she never spared his attention for even a fraction of second except the nights. Her attire, her gestures and her voice seemed to be exercised in harmony only to imprison his masculine urge. He might have felt the uncanny change but was simply overpowered by the hypnotic spell cast by her enigmatic appeal. One evening, he suggested in nervous tone, "I feel, you no longer need to work day in and day out." Saying this he stopped to see her reaction anxiously. She could read his fear of disturbing the delicate tenderness in their relation. For some reason he was not ready to let it bear even a minor scratch.

She stared at him contemplatively but said nothing.

He gathered some more courage and said, "I mean...if I buy a house for you in... say another city a couple of hundred kilometers away where we are setting up our second factory...we can spend our time there more freely. Also...this rumour is spoiling your image as well as mine..."

She measured the intention for a long moment and said, "It's your image to be specific. You know I have no body in this world to care for."

"I am there..."

She smirked scornfully.

He said earnestly "I am there for you and I do care for your image as much as I do for mine. It's just the family..."

"So...you want me to live in another city!"

"I'll buy a nice apartment for you. There will be a car at your door step. Whenever you want do whatever, you can do. These things will be in your name not mine."

"But who am I? A mistress?"

"I don't know who you are for me...but please don't use such harsh words

on yourself. Only I don't know what you are not for me."

"I'll tell you what I am not for you...I am not your wife."

He fell silent for a long moment and then said, "It's just the family..."

"It's not 'just the family'...it's 'only the family'"

"Then tell me what should I do? If my wife finds out once more she will leave me."

"Then leave her...make me your family...leave her right now...today!"

"But my son..."

She did not answer and remained quiet.

After a few days she shifted her base to the new plush apartment two hundred kilometers away. One evening when she was taking a lazy walk in the nearby park, suddenly she heard a female voice calling her by her name. The voice seemed to have traveled a very long way before reaching her. She first felt that it was an illusion and did not respond but the voice rang once more and this time from a source quite close.

She turned to encounter a face left behind several years ago round the corner of a dingy ladies hostel. It was the girl from the small town who bailed her out of the torment of her cousin and led her to the riddles on this new life.

It was a pleasant surprise for her. She hardly knew anyone in the city. Due to the development of the disapproving relation with her employer, she had consciously stayed away from everyone she knew earlier.

"Oh! Nice apartment." her friend remarked while taking her place in front of the wide window on the southern wall.

She watched her impressed, "You dress so simple but still look so beautiful!"

"Well...I can't afford very expensive clothes," her friend smiled. By the way, what are you doing lately?"

She was expecting this question coming and was considering different options as her reply. Finally she decided to tell her a lie. But, once confronted with the question, she ended up saying, "Nothing."

"Nothing!" her friend said incredulously.

"Well…since you know my stories partly, I think I can tell you the remaining part till date. It's a chain of mistakes…but when you listen you will be as confused as I am today about who really committed those mistakes…perhaps only few could be attributed to me but majority...I have no idea. And, I don't know how to stop doing any more blunders either..."

"Please carry on. I think, I land up in your life always at the right time…only those few hundred rupees you borrowed during the train journey are still due! And…that's the reason I had to dig you out finally from this remote corner of the earth," her friend said jokingly.

"If that's the reason you hunted me out, then I shall neither pay that to you now so that you keep on running after me forever and whenever I need you, you will emerge from nowhere!" she said.

"Now, tell me your story…only get me a cup of tea…that herbal tea without milk if you don't mind. I saw that in your kitchen."

"Of course…" she went to the kitchen and put some water to boil while starting to tell her the details of her life so far.

She narrated everything with brutal honesty. Her friend absorbed each word with rapt attention and concern.

After she was through, it was late and the clock on the wall ticked eight at night. In between, he called her thrice and became intrigued more and more after every call when he was informed that she was busy chatting with an old friend of hers. He had not heard much about that friend. In fact he had been so engrossed in her physical aspect all those years that there was barely any scope of peeking into any other side. He could not believe that she could have a friend also…any other living being also in this world that she knew other than him.

Finally when she was through with her story, her friend remained quiet for a long time and said, "I think I must go now but I shall come back soon.

This time it's me who will come back and perhaps you will not want"

She was surprised "What do you mean by that?"

Her friend smiled cryptically, "You will realize later why I said that, not now."

"Where do you live? You have not said much about your own life."

"Some other day. But there is not much that I can speak about. I live in a rented apartment not far from here. It's a small flat. I live alone there. Now I must hurry because there is a heap of exam papers I have to check."

"You are teaching in this primary school, right?"

"Yes. Side by side I am also attached to an organization doing social work. That's all and this job does not give me much money. Hence the small rented apartment."

"I never understood why you have not married yet!"

"Oh...I can't explain really why; but I have gone through a few relationships over the past years. But I never understood what commitment is. Men and women want to run into a false pretence of committing to each other for a lifetime. It's kind of challenging the laws of nature! Forget it. I said I shall come back soon. Bye for now."

She watched from the nineteenth floor window as the serene disposition of her friend wrapped in a simple white sari and embellished with only one black framed spectacle disappeared round the corner. The composed and unattached deportment somehow commanded respect and envy both in her mind. She did not know if she wanted to meet her friend again but the promise of coming back sounded like a warning she was frightened to face.

He arrived unannounced in the morning.

"Who was that?"

"Oh! That was an old friend of mine who brought me to you," she said mischievously.

"Come on, don't talk in riddles." He looked intrigued.

She explained in some detail and he was convinced.

Then followed some amorous days and nights.

After lunch, they went to the nearby coffee shop.

An old couple was sitting at the next table. There was a small baby boy of about one and half years of age. The baby was raising hell around him. It was becoming very difficult for the old lady to control him. At times he would shake the delicate designer table with both his hands and the glasses quivered on the verge of toppling. The old man in a fit of anxiety grabbed the almost falling objects. Then at times the baby would try to push the empty chairs savagely and turn them upside down with the intention of causing noise. The couple was extremely anxious but seemed to be used to that. So far it was only bit noisy but there was no other problem.

Suddenly the baby left the hand of the old man and darted towards her. She was nibbling with a small piece of pastry just served on her table. As the toddler almost reached near her, she noticed the progress and smiled indulgently. In a strange move, the baby held her by her knee and scrambled to climb onto her lap. She, slightly taken aback, lifted him on her lap and made him sit. In the mean time the old man rose to his feet and rushed to get the child back. She said politely "It's all right," and tried to hand over the child. And then the trouble started. The baby would not release its clutch. He held a part of her dress tightly and would not let it go. He adamantly refused to leave her. The old man desperately tried to persuade the baby to come back with him but without any effect. Finally as the old man forcefully pulled him apart from her, the baby started crying hysterically. They took the baby back to their place and tried to divert his attention towards cakes and pastries in the showcase a few feet away. Nothing worked and the baby kept on crying desperately turning his face towards her.

"Bring him to me…" she said and took the baby on her lap again. Instantly the baby stopped crying and remained silent wrapping his small cute hands around her neck and resting his head on her shoulder as if some long lost comfort was suddenly found. It was strange.

She could not finish her coffee. He was also surprised at this turn of events. The baby's unexpected fondness was a mystery. After a while, the old couple paid the bill and was ready to leave. The baby seemed to have already slept in her lap. The old lady came forward and took the baby from her.

"Very sweet boy," said she.

"You know what?" said the old woman.

She stared quizzically.

"This is our grandson and we lost our daughter a year ago. There is a strange similarity between you and our daughter. I think he mistook you as his mother; that's why he was not leaving you."

Her smile disappeared and she could not say a word. She drew near the baby and kissed him on his soft flabby cheeks. The baby was fast asleep by then.

The old man was looking in another direction seemingly haunted by the pain of loss refreshed by her uncanny similarity.

"You are a nice couple. I don't know if you have a baby of yours already but your baby would be as sweet as this one. God bless you!" They left the coffee shop.

They also finished their coffee and left after few moments.

He planned to stay there for few days at a stretch. The second factory was in the making. He had to supervise the construction work.

The afternoon rolled into evening and evening became night. The mystique darkness hung from the sky. Gusts of wind hurtled down the hill several miles away and stomped onto the small bungalows and cottages before rushing into her bedroom. He was busy that day due to incessant telephone calls from the site. So their conversation was rather interrupted and not so much intense as on other days.

He was explaining, "I shall have to build a canteen you know. There is a government law that says that canteen is mandatory if you build a factory employing more than certain number of employees. In my case this number is quite large."

She half listened to what was said.

He went on, "Do you think there should be a non-vegetarian section in the canteen?"

She did not respond and stared at the dark horizon unmindfully.

"Are you listening?"

"I want a baby," suddenly she said turning her face flushed with resolute determination.

He was not prepared for this and looked perplexed.

"You heard it right. I want a baby and that's going to be your child," she repeated coldly.

He now understood the proposition clearly. After a moment's thought he said, "That's not a good idea. It will create a mess both for you and for me in the future."

She glared at him and said, "Why? I could neither get the status of a legal member of the society because you wanted to stick to your so called wife and now I shall have to be deprived of the pleasure of being a mother! No...I can't lose everything a woman deserves and you enjoy all possible goodness from both relations. You must marry me and get me a child...you must."

He was at a complete loss and fumbled for words, "Look...I explained to you before that it's my son whose life is at stake and I can't spoil his future for my happiness."

She was now agitated and said sarcastically, "That's a good excuse. Actually you know what? Half your stories are all humbug. You are having as much sex with that bitch as with me. You are a mere pervert. You want both women to feed your carnal hunger and nothing else."

He was visibly upset with this crude attack. "Don't talk like that. What have I not done for your comfort, have you ever thought? Is marriage everything? And so long the question of my relation with my wife is concerned, I said before also, we don't share the same bed from that day itself."

"Then what does she share with you? Why? Why can't you even think of leaving her and marrying me?" she almost screamed in frustration.

He said, "She shares my son with me and you know that."

She did not react for some time and finally asked calmly with an undercurrent of cold warning, "So...you will not marry me."

He remained silent and the silence asserted his denial.

After a few seconds she rose to her feet and slowly left the room. She entered into the second bedroom and locked the door from inside.

And...it was then that she gulped a handful of sleeping pills.

The bell rang and she went to open the door. It was her friend standing with her serene smile hanging at the corner of her thin and delicate lips. As usual there was no suggestion of any make up on her face except the only ornament, the black rimmed spectacle snugly set on the nose. She watched her friend in amazement and wondered how she held some kind of iron strength behind the façade of feminine softness and that too without any external make up.

Her friend made her own tea and asked her to relax. With her cup of herbal tea she settled on a chair next to the window and said calmly, "So...you wanted to die?"

She smiled uncomfortably and finally said, "No. I wanted to live."

"And you felt that death was the way to life?"

She had no answer. After a long silence she started narrating what transpired over the past few days.

Finally, her friend asked curiously, "Do you really want to marry him?"

She was taken aback by this question. The immediate response was going to be "Of course, I do," but somehow something held her tongue. She stayed silent and her friend spoke in a tone as if she was reading from the shady alleys in her mind. "Actually, you just want to win. We all want to either win or don't want to lose. His wife would never be ready to lose and you are trying to win. But, the irony remains hidden in the fact that in the process of this war we end up forgetting the worth of the cause. Is the object worth your die hard struggle? And…love! That's more elusive than real. Do you know what he loves? You think he loves his wife and his wife thinks it's you who has cornered all his love. No. Believe me he loves his security and peace and that's why, he does not want to leave the family. On the other hand, he loves the excitement he gets from adventure and sex. Hence, he keeps you in his life. He needs both. Now if we consider his wife, you think she loves him so much that she would become a nun or something if he deserts her? Come on…it's her pride and ego. It's the society that must not know that she failed to keep her husband captivated by her charm. It has nothing to do with her love for him. She sure hates him by now. So, you see, both of you are running after different goals but still somehow colliding with each other in a strange way.

I tell you there is a common misunderstanding. Why do you want him to marry you? He is there for you anyway…what more will you get from marriage? Commitment…right? You think he is so powerful that he can commit? None of us are really. None! Why do we feel better when we live in these large concrete houses like the one you are living in now? That floor made of solid marble, that wall made of granite and these thick wooden window frames…yes…they offer a kind of assurance of longevity, or in some way, a kind of commitment. But that's fooling our own selves. I can tell you, this area used to be a marshy land infested with snakes and other wild insects. Those insects were so secure in that sludge of dirt and mud that they felt nothing could ever destroy them. But one day the large dumpers and bull dozers changed the face of the earth here. Today I am sitting by this window sipping herbal tea! May be who knows…some time later the insects and snakes would be back. So…where does your security stand? It's as unstable as insecurity."

She listened with rapt attention and felt that the words were able to touch some unseen unused chord in her heart and mind. She mumbled, "He wants to take me to Switzerland."

Her friend said, "How does that change your life? Don't be like the kite that flies in the sky with its string rooted on the ground and finally it comes back to the same old gray dust. Instead, look at the stars. They never come down and always float in the sky. You know what? Material pleasure is like swigs of alcohol. The more you drink…the more you get drunk and the less you realize the degree of your drunkenness. At the end there is indigestion. The pleasure turns into bitterness.

She listened but said nothing. Finally her friend checked her watch and decided to leave. She went up to the door and stopped for a moment. "There is a vacancy in my school. The salary is small but that does not matter. You can be happy any day you choose to be. Happiness is not hidden somewhere in your future husband or your possible child but it's within yourself. If you look for a book in a grocery store, you will never get. You should look for the right thing in the right place."

Her friend left repeating the information that there was a vacancy for a school teacher in the primary section once more. She stood at the doorway silently. Life seemed to be throwing some flash on some unseen arena. She needed to do some thinking. At least the new images did not look as grim and ominous as the ones few hours ago.

The brooding evening

His wife stood at the window for a long time. The sun almost went down the western horizon and the sky turned red. The kiss felt good. She could not remember exactly how long back she had experienced this in her married life. That evening when she left their bed room in a rage stating that they would no more sleep together, the last thread had snapped without any noise. Later on she often felt that she should not have done that in a fit of anger. Rather she might have been more diplomatic that day. Instead of trying to exact an immediate revenge, she should have mounted a slow and insidious attack on the real enemy. More and more she pondered over the whole thing, she felt that her husband had some role to play undoubtedly, but he became like a victim of circumstances. Perhaps he was no more in his rational control. By driving him away harshly, she was actually making the job of that female easy. He was naturally seeking comfort in her company.

The kiss was unethical. It was beyond the approval of social norm. But at the end, it felt good. She thought, "Well, generally accepted social guidelines or viewpoints are set with a purpose of enabling a better life but then there are imperfections. To fit into an imperfect cavity, one must be imperfect. So, life often falls beyond the assumptions made by the makers of social norms and hence the existing guidelines fail to take care of the events outside its realm."

As she thought of her husband she found a difference between him and her. Both came on the same platform today, yet, there was a difference. He bought misery and pleasure with his money and power and for her life was leading her blindfolded. She could only walk without much deliberation.

She went to the kitchen to oversee the preparation of the dinner. There were some lobsters in the kitchen. They were purchased almost seven days back. Her husband bought that last week. She had lost her enthusiasm about eating various kinds of dishes lately. Hence, the lobsters were not cooked. They were washed, cleaned and kept in the deep freeze. She pulled out the tray and found the lobsters to be frozen very hard and sticking adamantly to the plastic base. She kept it outside by the side of the kitchen platform to soften. The maidservant noticed the lobsters and looked at her curiously. She felt her stare and asked, "Want to ask something?"

"No…just like that!"

She was not convinced, "You want to ask something…ask"

"Who will eat so much? Do you think uncle will have dinner tonight?"

She felt irritated at this. Even the maidservant knew that he had dinner outside most of the nights. She could not find a suitable reply to shut her up as well as vent her frustration.

"We shall eat."

"So much!"

"You don't have to think much and just do as I say."

The maid servant went on with her job of chopping the vegetables.

She checked the stock and nodded with satisfaction that all the special and rare spices were available at her disposal. She decided to prepare a coastal dish. It's been almost a month that she never did something like that. In fact, most of the time, she boiled rice and some vegetables in the pressure cooker and somehow passed them down her throat. The maid servant had been there for a long time in the house and knew the very taste of every member. Once in a while she dared to point out, "Uncle would not like that. Let's cook something better for him."

In fact once she expressed her opinion that he was eating outside because the quality of food at home had lost its thrill for him. She fired her left and right at this crossing of the limit of authority. She reminded the girl that it was not her business at all.

Today she decided to pour all her skill to prepare the special coastal dish. After a long time, cooking gave a kind of kick to her mind. She felt invigorated. Shortly the house was filled with the aroma. From the smell she knew that the dish was in right direction. It had to be. There cannot be a slip today. After all, she was applying her mind to this after a very long time. Once she used to be a master in this. So many gatherings took place in that very hall in the past whenever her husband struck a big business deal. He invited many of his employees and held his party. The food was never brought from outside but always cooked by her and the guests left applauding about the mouth watering taste and flavor. Those days have faded into oblivion but she still knew how to cast a spell through her culinary skill. The food was almost prepared and she went to the dining room to make a telephone call.

The telephone on the other end was ringing. After several rings, the call was responded by an answering machine: "I am not at home. Please leave your message."

She dialed the number of the cell phone and this time it was answered immediately "Hi…is everything okay?"

"Yes…where are you? I tried your home but you are not there!"

"I just left."

"Come back for dinner. I have prepared some special coastal dish of lobster for you. You would love it."

"Oh...no! I can't come."

"Why?" she was surprised and slightly withdrawn immediately.

"This afternoon I got a call from office. There was an emergency at some other site that needed my immediate attention. Since there was nothing to do at home I left. By the way, has he arrived?"

"No. Not yet."

She was upset but tried not to show much of her feeling and asked indifferently, "When are you expected back?"

"Say in another fifteen days. You eat my share as well this time."

She looked at the wall clock. It's pretty late at night. Her husband should have been back by now. He called around seven hours back. The interview was scheduled the next day. She tried to convince herself that there might be traffic on the way but the reasoning did not appeal much. Though she wanted to avoid the bitter thought of the other woman, yet, the possibility of his going back to her place poked her mind. Though he had tried to keep it a secret the news had reached her that he had bought a house and settled her in the town where he was setting up his second factory. The moment she thought of the other woman she lost her cool composure. She was no more on a philosophical plane. The fulfillment of the kiss evaporated in a blink and she became agitated again. How dare he compromise the meeting at the school tomorrow just for the sake of that bitch. She wanted a showdown. She would ask him point blank, if he scrapped his family completely. May be he was at the moment having an amorous moment in the arms of that dirty female yet he must answer her questions.

She almost jabbed the buttons of the telephone key pad and waited for an answer. The line sounded busy at first and then she made another attempt. Her facial muscle tightened, brows knitted, lips pursed.

This time the telephone was ringing. She held the receiver tight against her ear. She would not leave a single loose end today. She prepared herself for the lashing torrent of sharp words. Her mind was racing at a furious pace…but as she finished her mental preparation, she noticed with surprise that the other end was still ringing. There was no response. She waited as long as it rang and finally the line was disconnected automatically. She tried once more and this time also there was no response!

She stood there exasperated. She concluded bitterly, "He is not taking my call. Okay!"

She asked the maidservant to take her son to the bed. The sumptuous dinner was waiting in the kitchen. She felt like throwing the whole thing into the waste bin. She did not have any more appetite left in her. She put aside some portion of it in a bowl for the maidservant and placed the rest into the refrigerator. Suddenly she felt very tired. She went to her bedroom and lay on the bed and stared at the ceiling blankly.

What went wrong?

In the hotel room he downed his third peg of whisky and pushed the glass aside. The glass knocked an empty beer bottle which toppled from the table. It fell on the ground but did not break. He once again set it straight on the ground near the wall. Then he pulled the heavyset sofa next to the air conditioner and sat on it facing the chilled air.

The tandoori chicken was really good. The meat was soft and well marinated. The crab and lobster were yet to appear on his table. He fumbled for the receiver to order another whisky.

The blistering hot noon passed at a painfully slow pace. At last the sun turned red and sank into the western horizon. The stinging heat was adamant, blatantly refusing to go down with the sun. Finally a velvety darkness solemnly descended on the wilderness. Dumb silence engulfed the landscape. The shed almost ceased to exist and vanished in the black night because the only bulb was not switched on today. The boy preferred to keep it dark because the man was asleep. He did not want to disturb his rest. The boy understood that the man would not eat tonight as well but hunger was looming large in the boy's stomach. Sitting with his back rested against the side of the bed he dozed off. Suddenly when he woke up, he realized that it was quite late and he must go to the food mall in search of some food. He got up and checked the condition of the man who appeared to be lost deep in slumber.

The boy started his walk towards the food mall which was the only sign of life flickering on the earth. In fact the food mall never slept. The boy walked cautiously along the side of the dark highway. Speeding cars and trucks as well as busses zoomed from the darkness like raging monsters and again vanished into the black night. They would not get a chance to stop in case someone came on their way. So, the boy had to be careful not to interfere with the business of motion.

As the boy arrived at the food mall, it did not look like a flickering flame any more but seemed to be vibrant with festive mood. It was always like that even in the middle of the night. There was no dearth of nocturnal travelers and there was no end of hunger. Even at that odd hour, it was bustling with crowd. They ate, refreshed and followed their mission with steadfast resolve. The food courts were geared to serve as quick as possible. The essence was speed. Nobody was expected to come back the next day again and there were not many options around. Hence the price was high. Men and women in a hurry did not mind that bit of extra payment but just enjoyed the short relaxation after a prolonged time behind the wheel. The boy liked the atmosphere in some way though he knew he was not a part of them. The shed and the food mall were stationary while the rest of the world moved. They came and went. The boy knew he was a part of the stationary thing. That's why he was never in a hurry like the man or like the mountains. In fact, once the man told the boy about the highway. From that day the boy envied the highway. The endless winding highway never went anywhere but stayed fixed in its root yet it witnessed everything...from one end of the earth to the other. It witnessed the roaring vehicles with gasping engines running in frenzy and then breaking down under stress, collapsing under burden...but the highway never moved a bit. So, the boy learnt to admire the concrete road that beat them all in its reach.

In the food mall, the boy had to locate the waiter who generally had a stock of stolen leftovers. The waiter was few years older than the boy and due to some unknown reason he shared whatever he could sneak out from the kitchen during the day.

As their eyes met, the waiter indicated the boy to wait. After placing the tray in hand on the assigned table, he went inside the kitchen. After a little while he came out from there with an impassive face. The boy knew where to look. The waiter had a long hidden pocket in his trouser and the stolen food was stashed there. Though the trouser was loose enough not to bulge the boy's eyes never missed. In a single glance the boy knew where it was hidden and which day went lucky for the waiter. Today, it was not much. As the waiter walked out almost unnoticed from the eating area, the boy followed him. They met at a place outside the crowded mall.

"What do you have today? I am hungry," asked the boy.

"I don't have much today. The manager was around most of the time." He delved into the depth of his pocket and pulled out a sandwich and one packet full of cold French fries. The boy watched the pocket from outside.

"You still have something. What is that?" insisted the boy.

The waiter smiled mischievously and slowly pulled out another golden color packet arousing great suspense.

The boy saw the packet and tried to snatch it from him in curiosity. The waiter quickly swung his hand to take it away from the boy's reach. "This is a cigarette packet. Some one left it on a table. Almost full you see..." He opened the lid and showed the contents to the boy who took a quick peek into it and anxiously looked around if any one saw them.

"You smoke?" asked the boy apprehensively.

"Not really...but I got this free. Only once in a while I do. In the past, I smoked regularly when there was another manager. That fellow used to share his cigarettes with me. After he left I almost stopped. Now I shall have one." the waiter held one cigarette between his lips and flicked a matchstick against the matchbox. The flame was quickly snuffed out due to wind. On the third attempt the tip of the cigarette turned fluorescent red and the waiter pulled a long drag but released almost immediately through the crack between his lips. The boy watched the smoke gushing out through his mouth and nostril. After a few drags, the waiter almost closed his eyes as if he was deeply absorbed cherishing the charm of the flavor. Suddenly he said, "You know…I can do something special. Look now."

He indicated the boy to follow him next to the wall where the flow of wind was less. He filled his mouth with smoke and slowly released the same in the form of rings. The rings floated in the stillness of the air for a few moments and then diffused. After watching him for a few moments, the boy hesitantly said, "Do you mind sharing that one with me? I have never had a smoke!"

The waiter started laughing and said, "You? You are a boy…you want to smoke!"

The boy was embarrassed, "I just wanted to taste…that's it"

The waiter removed the cigarette from his lips and held that out in front of the boy. "Okay…go ahead. Take it. Try this one."

The boy held the cigarette between his teeth and almost bit it. The waiter screamed, "Oh…stop it. You will spoil it!"

He showed the boy how to hold it between his lips and then the boy pulled a long drag. As soon as the smoke made its way through his throat, he started coughing convulsively. The burning cigarette slipped off the lips and the boy's face turned crimson in exhaustion. The waiter patted his back and took the cigarette back. As the boy calmed down, the waiter teased, "I told you…this is not for boys but for men."

The boy was panting and said haltingly, "Okay…okay…it was horrible. You give me the sandwich and the French fries."

After finishing the food, the boy asked, "Why don't you light another cigarette and blow those rings in the air. That's very funny."

The waiter agreed and he started blowing rings in the air. The boy watched a few times and then kept following the path of the ring trying to run his fingers through the hollow in the centre of the rings. Every time he could do that, he giggled in pleasure. The giggle of the boy sunk into the bustle of the crowd. It was not a problem because nobody had time to bother about the game the boy was playing with the rings of smoke in the middle of the night.

The crab was superb. The lobsters turned out to be really fresh and succulent. The whisky did its job. He decided to pay a visit to the ATM now. The clock just struck ten. He was about to scramble out of the room when his mobile phone started to ring. He realized that he was almost oblivious of his belongings. The ring of the mobile phone reminded him that he did not even collect his money bag before leaving. The money bag was lying half open on the table with a few coins sprawled on the wooden base. He went and picked up the phone but the haze of alcohol did not allow him to read the caller's number clearly. He brought it close to his eyes. It was from a person who used to be his friend one day. A soul very close to his heart. But…but not today. Today they were separated by a mountain. He wondered, "Why is he calling at this hour! It must be another one of his sermons about family life and so called responsibility. I have to listen to all that crap from a person who never had a family of his own!" He stared at the vibrating cell phone for a long time indecisively. He could not decide if he should take the call or not. His mind heavily intoxicated by spirit raced back two decades ago.

It was a function in the Engineering College. In the college lexicon, it was called fest. The fest was organized once every year. It was a grand bash for two weeks with various kinds of cultural functions taking place throughout the day. Students from the engineering college and other colleges in the city thronged the multiple auditoriums. Apart from the attraction of live songs, drama, quiz or other cultural activities, there was always the well publicized excitement about the possibility of starting a new affair. There could be occasions for girls and boys to interact. So, everyone expected to strike a romantic encounter during those fourteen days.

That evening there was a music program in the open theatre. A famous band was invited to perform on stage. That band, unlike all others of those days, did not only mince words against the social stagnation and fantasies about unscrupulous government employees but also crooned love songs. They played both type of roles, the role of romantics as well as the role of angry young men. Hence, everyone got something of choice from the menu. The audience was in high spirits. Generally, the girls bunched together at certain spots whereas the boys were spread all over with the exception of few couples already formed during some previous fest.

He was among the male crowd and was having a ball of a time participating in the hoot and jeer. There were a host of food stalls lined up by the side of the compound. Some one or the other ensured a continuous supply of snacks from there. He had his share of fried nuts and was about to pass it on to the person standing next to him but realized that there was nothing left in the cone shaped paper sack. He listened to the songs and unmindfully kept folding the paper. After a while he found that the paper had turned out to be a toy plane. As the song was over, in an excited outburst, he threw the paper plane in the air. The folded piece of paper sailed high in the air and after traveling a short distance prepared for a smooth landing. Shortly, it was moving with its nose heading downward. By that time another song started. The guitarist with very clumsy unkempt bunch of hair was almost on the verge of tearing the strings of his Spanish guitar. The singers were about to destroy their vocal cord by shouting on top of their might. He was lost in the high pitched outburst of music and it was then that the paper plane made its smooth landing right at the delicate cleavage of a very buxom girl of second year English honors. In fact, he felt that his duty was over as soon as he let the plane take off from his hand and hence he did not concern himself about its safe landing. He was jolted back to senses when a robust palm slammed against his cheeks. His spectacles snapped and got displaced. One of the glasses broke and a small broken fragment stuck to his flesh. The right eye narrowly escaped a fatal injury. There was blood on his face. For a moment he was stupefied and then tried to understand what went wrong. In the mean time another blow hit him on the right shoulder. He fell on the ground and saw another student standing in front of him like a lion on the prowl boiling in anger. He was feeling faint, when he heard the reason he was being beaten black and blue: "How dare you outrage her modesty!" And then everything was black. He fainted.

When he came to, he was in the bed of the college hospital. There were several anxious faces crowding around him. As the hazy images crystallized into distinct shapes, he felt a kind of pride of victory along with anxiety. He stared at all of them and faintly said, "I am fine…"

Someone said, "We gave him back what he deserved. He was a stupid chap from Production Engineering Department. How he dared to touch you we never know. That evening itself, we trapped him after the show near the second gate and bashed him to the extent that he almost died on the spot. I think he has a few bones unbroken."

He thought for a moment and asked, "How about the girl?"

"Oh! That fool was trying to impress her by acting smart."

"You mean she was not his girlfriend?"

"Not at all! In fact she already has a boyfriend who is anyway a hunk with large biceps and no brain."

"Where is he now?"

"He is recovering in the hospital."

The girl who was at the centre of the storm considered neither of them! She spent her free time behind the college canteen with another man. And, after this incident, their erotic encounters were well publicized.

This brought the perpetrator and the victim together as both of these men realized each other's fate with a caustic smirk. One day the whole fiasco fizzled out. They became friends. Very close friends.

Then, the four-year engineering course came near the finishing line. All the major companies of the country swarmed the campus. Every day multiple interviews were conducted simultaneously. Those days engineers were in short supply and hence there was a mad rush to book them in advance. There used to be an edgy crowd always gathered inside the office of the employment co-coordinator. Students were short-listed according to their academic records as well as the preference of the recruiters. Ironically, when the best of the academicians expected to bag the best jobs, the real outcomes turned out to be almost opposite. The most outgoing extrovert ones got the best placement. Some of the students got more than one job at a time. Some still waited for their luck to smile. In this situation, he could not strike a quick success and was becoming anxious with every passing day. His friend was through with his first placement already.

"The new list has come out; have you seen?" asked his friend one day while sitting in the college canteen smoking a cheap cigarette.

He failed to get through a number of times before and was curious immediately, "Am I there in it?"

"Yes. I am not there. This is for the company who is known to be the highest pay master in the campus. And you know what... they are a launching pad. Once you start your career from there, your bio data will become a craze in the future"

"Who else are there?"

"Oh never bother about it. I have checked all the names. The other contenders are no match for you."

"Why are you not short-listed in it? Have you checked with the placement officer?"

"No. I did not. I think they are trying to avoid one student getting two jobs."

"But this is the best job...had you not been selected earlier, you would have got a chance."

"That's true. Anyway...I wish that you get through this one then your career will really take off."

The next morning, he wore his best shirt and trouser. The tie was borrowed from his friend with the know how of tying the knot. After a number of futile attempts of keeping the narrow end of the tie smaller than the broader frontal part, his friend had to literally do the tying. Finally he looked almost like an executive. His friend made a final check and nodded approvingly.

As he arrived at the conference room, the situation was surprising. At least five short-listed candidates out of fifteen were not present for the pre-placement talk. After the introduction was over, the interviewer said, "I find few candidates missing. I request you to please get some of your friends who might be interested in these openings. We shall start our process of interview after an hour."

The students filed out of the conference room wondering whom to present that rare chance. He had no qualm in his mind about whom to talk to. He did not waste any time and went straight to the canteen where his friend was generally found during the class timings.

"Come with me. There is a shortfall and they wanted us to call our friends for appearing in the interview."

His friend was savoring a cup of hot tea with one of his cheap cigarettes. The taste of the tea was stale due to the use and re-use of same tea leaves. But no one actually cared about it because the spirit of youth was so high that they barely had the patience to bother about the subtlety of taste of the brown colored liquid.

His friend was in a mood of absolute relaxation that morning and did not even stir at this piece of information. He insisted once more, "Now move...come. You don't need to be short-listed...just come for the interview."

His friend now smiled casually and said, "I can't. Don't you see my attire today? I did not even shave this morning. I look shabby. It's madness to even try to appear for an interview in this condition."

"You have a point but they know that one can't be in fine clothes all the time." He pulled his friend by his hand. "Come...get up!"

His friend rose to his feet hesitantly and after a moment's deliberation he decided to meet the placement officer who was an experienced senior professor. The placement officer stared at his face for a long time with a mischievous smile and finally said, "I think you have a fair chance of getting this job. Please go ahead."

They headed for the central building where the interview was scheduled.

The panel called one candidate after the other and grilled them with various kinds of strange queries. He had prepared with great care over the past seven days trying to cover all possible aspect. When his turn came he proceeded with a pulsating heart.

After a long discussion about his family background and other general things, they announced that they would now discuss the technical side. He nodded. This side was rather easy for him.

"So what is your favorite subject?"

"Fluid mechanics"

"Good...let's start with Archimedes theory"

It was too simple for him and he was very confident. The discussion went on at a smooth pace. He knew he was doing well. In fact, very well.

After a long session on Archimedes theorem, the queries slowly started becoming tougher. He managed to come up with his answers that were often innovative but sometimes unsure. He gauged from the expressions of the people in front of him that he was doing fine when he suddenly turned nervous. And it was then that the simplest question landed in front of him.

"What is the value of Reynolds-number for transition from laminar to turbulent flow?"

He knew the answer by heart but suddenly it was lost. He fell silent as if his mind was asleep. He gaped blankly at their expectant faces. The question was repeated and finally the answer rolled out of his mouth.

The interview was over. He walked out of the room completely confused. There was something drastically wrong but it was not clear to him. Next was the turn of his friend who went in with a very casual air. After about fifteen minutes his friend came out with a smiling face.

"They found me funny," he said, "They just had a casual chat and did not ask a single serious question! After sometime, they told me to leave and I left.

He could not join the laughter and dragged his friend out of the crowded lawn.

Once they were out of the building he narrated the whole conversation that took place with him during the interview. His friend listened to him with rapt attention and commented that he should be selected at any rate.

But after a moment's silence his friend almost shrieked, "What did you say in reply to that Reynolds number?"

"Why? Twenty thousand...!" and immediately his face turned white in frustration. "Oh no! How could I say that!"

"Indeed! How could you say that! You taught hydraulics to the whole class and you made this silly mistake! How?"

He sat on the railing by the side of the walkway and hid his face in his palms. After a long silence he said painfully, "I don't know why I uttered twenty thousand instead of two thousand! What will happen? They are sure to reject me!"

His friend did not answer but looked worried. The rest of the day they spoke little and most of the time stared at the sky. The result was expected to be announced in the evening.

They brooded the whole day and in the evening with anxious anticipation both of them went to meet the placement officer. He was concerned for himself and his friend was anxious for him. As soon as they appeared at the doorstep, the old man stood up and addressed his friend with an excited voice, "Please come, gentleman. I told you that you would make it! And you know what? You have got the job. It's all my gut feeling. My senses never go wrong. You see these white hairs?" He pointed his finger at his white hair. "These are not white for nothing. I knew the first thing in the morning as soon as I saw you that you were going to strike. And you did. They selected three candidates and you are one of those three. Congratulations!"

He wanted to ask if he was also one of the three but somehow could not. His friend was also taken aback at this outcome and was dumbfounded. After a long time he mumbled, "What about him?"

The professor quickly glanced at him and shook his head sadly. He rushed out of the room and started walking back to the hostel while pulling his tie viciously.

"Please wait...I am coming," his friend desperately called him from behind and ran to catch up with him. Once they were together his friend looked at his face pensively and almost apologetically said, "I am so sorry!"

He turned and looked at his friend's face, "Come on! What are you sorry for! It's my misfortune. There were other two guys who got selected. I am incapable and hence I lost it. Why should you be sorry?"

"I never wanted to come. I killed your chance. I...I don't know what to do now!" his friend lamented.

"Nothing. Let's go, we shall celebrate your success tonight." His friend did not respond but silently walked side by side. They bought a quarter liter bottle of rum and drank that in steel glasses sitting on the lawn of the hostel that night. There was not much to talk. He was extremely frustrated and his

friend blamed himself for being lucky. The next day, he slept till late in the morning. Someone in the evening dropped information that the big company had a hidden list of selected candidates who would be recruited one by one in case the candidates from the first list refused to accept the offer. Little flicker of hope flashed in his mind but it was far too impossible anyway because their offer was extremely lucrative. The salaries and perks were much more than any other. Who would decline an offer like that?

The next morning also, he arrived at the college a little late missing the first session. But as soon as he stepped into the compound, one of the classmates flashed a broad smile at him and said, "At last! You hit the bull's eye!"

He looked at him totally confused, "What? What are you talking about?"

"You got the best job finally! Only four candidates got such a break. Well done buddy!"

He was still at a loss and asked with a puzzled look, "Of course they recruited four candidates but I am not one of those four!"

"You were not initially but one of the first four dropped out. He expressed his lack of desire to join them. You were the fifth one, it seems. Go to the placement office. There is a notice in this regard."

He ran towards the placement office and stood in front of the notice board. The board was protected by a cover of fine mesh of wire and the mesh was perhaps never cleaned. As a result the sieves became blocked with dust particles and dirt. He had to almost press his nose against the mesh and finally he found his name mentioned in the list of candidates selected. He checked the four names and found with dismay that one name was missing. It was his Friend who had dropped out!

He realized what had happened and quickly started walking towards the canteen.

"That's not fair," he said.

"What's not fair?" asked his friend with an impish grin.

"I don't like favors. I like to fight and win!" he said in excitement.

The smile now disappeared from the face of his friend and he stared at him with a frown, "Fight! You want to fight with me and win! I thought we were friends and we would never fight with each other!"

"Oh! I don't mean that. But why did you do this! It's too much!"

"It's not a very big sacrifice that I have made. I have another job and I just refused this one. Let's both be happy…come on!"

"But this one was with a better prospects."

"I know. But it was not possible to offer you the other job. Now … now smile."

"Can we make it in the same city you think?"

"I don't know. Neither of the companies has announced the place of posting. These are large corporate with offices all over the country. Let's see."

When the two companies sent the placement details, they discovered that they were posted to different places two thousand kilometers away from each other. As it always happens, the promise of keeping in touch reminded them to write letters to each other but the frequency went down gradually. One day, their past took shelter in their cherished memories. Often over a glass of whisky in tall glasses after office, they remembered the days left behind.

Years passed by and life sailed in its own rhythm. He stayed in that Company for some time and left for a better position of responsibility in another organization. All his contact numbers as well as addresses altered. One day he got married and started a new phase of his life.

One evening, he came home very tired. The whole day was a rigorous schedule of one meeting after the other. He wanted to sleep as soon as he arrived home. His wife had kept the dinner ready and he was having it like a zombie. It was then that the silence of his tenth floor flat got ruptured by loud singing from somewhere. He was surprised in the beginning.

"Who is that?" he asked his wife.

"I have no idea but there seems to be new neighbor next to us," his wife said with uncertainty.

"That's awful! Why is he shouting in the thick of the night? This is time to sleep!" he commented bitterly.

"Come on. He is singing. I think he has a good voice."

"At this hour? I can't sleep like that."

"It's not too late. It's only evening, my dear. You are tired and that's why you want to sleep."

"I see…but I don't quite like his yelling. That's not a song at any rate!"

"You have never found any song worth listening to. He is not to blame for that. Forget him. Just finish your dinner and go to sleep. The bed is ready."

He did not reply but kept on eating in silence. But the voice disturbed him badly. After finishing his dinner, he put on a T-shirt and told his wife, "I think I have to put a stop to that madness. I want to lie down peacefully. That noise is giving me a headache."

His wife was now anxious. "It's not so bad. Nobody in the building is objecting…why do you want to unnecessarily pick up a fight with a neighbor? After all, he is going to live next door. Just ignore him."

He waved his head frantically and proceeded towards the door.

He knocked two three times on the door but nobody responded at first. After some time the door slowly opened and he was all ready to express his frustration bluntly on the face of the man appearing from behind the door but turned completely dumbfounded. They stared at each other, with a stunned expression, for a long moment and finally almost jumped in excitement, "You…!!!"

That was his long lost friend.

"Since when have you started making that kind of noise?"

"That's not noise. That's music. I love to sing. But tell me, how many years has it been since we parted at the railway station?"

"Not less than ten years! My goodness…I just can't imagine this could happen." All his tiredness and sleep vanished immediately. He invited his friend to his house and they started chatting like old days.

"This is my old friend. See...I spoke about him so much," he introduced his friend to his wife and she replied jokingly, "And he has been cursing you under his breath all the time after he came back home today. He said you were shouting!"

His friend started laughing, "I know. Actually due to this lack of artistic taste I smashed his nose many years back."

"Ah...I see. What about that girl of second year English honors? And...then the bashing by the mechanical army?"

They both broke into laughter.

"Where have you been all these years?"

"This is my third job you could say."

"But I remember you started your career with the same organization."

"Yes, I did, but I left the country to work for another firm abroad, and now again I'm back in the country staying the company flat next to yours." That evening he went to bed well past mid night.

They met almost every other evening and shared their life with each other. His wife also became a party in a short time. After a few pegs of whisky their spirits would be high and the conversation would roll onto another plane.

"Let's try Rum tomorrow like we used to drink in the college days."

"Rum! You know what? Today somehow Rum does not fit in my taste. I prefer whisky. This is the habit I picked up after so many office parties."

"Oh! Rum is value for money. Every swig gives its own share of high. That's why it was so popular during the college days. In fact I still prefer Rum. That's what I generally drink when I am alone."

"Don't tell me now that you want to try Rum in steel glasses with dents all over!"

"Oh, yes! You are right. We used to drink in steel glasses and sometime back in the evening at home I found all the glasses dirty and I thought, I could try steel glass once more. It's such a horrible taste I swear. The metallic

taste with spirit turns out to be a strange combination. Life has changed so much over the years."

"Hey...what did you do all these years tell me. You were living in that south-eastern country, right?"

"Yeah! That's right"

"What did you see?"

"I saw rain forest."

"Oh, come on...not rain forest now, please."

"What? You think rain forests are not worth seeing? Those forests are worth spending a life time in, I tell you."

"It has to be a worthless life like yours."

"No joking...you will never see such tall trees and strange insects elsewhere. In fact the jungle is so dense that even during the day time it's dark like night."

"Hmm...I understand...other than rain forest what else did you see?"

"Let me recall...I saw oil extraction rigs...offshore and on shore both."

"Now you are really irritating me...as bad as drinking rum from steel glass...please don't spoil the show. Tell me. Come on..."

"What? What do you expect...some angel or monster I have come across in that country like you read in fairy tales?"

"No. Not monsters. I mean angels...or fairies!"

"Hmm...now I know where you leading!"

"Then come out with it...fast!"

"Then listen. Yes...I have seen the karaoke bar...I have seen those rave parties or sandwich massages as well as wild personalized stripties."

"What...what? Karaoke bar?!!"

"Yes...in that the woman dances with you in a private room while shedding her precious clothes one by one and finally you can do whatever you like with her provided you have a hotel room in your reach."

"And the rave parties?"

"Ah...that was really funny! You never know when and where one would take place unless you get in touch with someone you know in that field. Once you book a ticket for that through that known person, he will take you to the venue."

"And then?"

"Then they give you a locker room. You have to remove all your clothes and keep them in the locker. After that a door opens and you enter into a big hall bursting with loud music where all the guests are naked like you...man or woman!"

"Huh! Deadly!"

"And...the funniest thing is a special kind of dinner."

"Dinner?"

"Yes! Several dishes are served on the table."

"What is so special?"

"Yes...they are all served on different erotic spots of a nude beautiful woman."

"My goodness! And...tell me the truth. Did you sleep with any of those females?"

His friend fell silent for a long moment and then said, "Yes...I did or I did not."

"What does that mean?"

"Those days I was extremely upset. I did not tell you earlier about this part of my life. Actually I used to work with my current company in the past but had to leave in disgrace three years ago because of an affair with a colleague of mine. My romantic link with her was not liked by the bosses and I had to leave on a bitter note. When I was abroad, one fine morning I got the news that she had got married."

"Oh!"

"Yes, and I felt rather disoriented those days. I did not know how to overcome my frustration and in that fit of frustration I drank heavily, smoked like mad, and visited such places many times. But you know what? After a few times I realized it only made me more frustrated. So I stopped visiting them."

"But...you are back to the same organization today!"

"Yes...I am. But you know what? Ironically she was supposed to be working under me as I was coming back."

"She reports to you now!"

"No. She resigned the day before I joined!"

A silence hung heavy in the air. After a while he broke the silence "Why don't you sing a Ghazal of your choice."

"Which one?"

He mentioned the specific Ghazal.

"You?!! You want to hear that one! I can't believe it. Are you sure?"

"Of course!"

His wife intercepted, "Do you know what he does during the leisure hours lately?" she said, looking at his face. He was smiling broadly.

"Listening to you, he has developed a taste for music and he bought dozens of cassettes. He plays them almost every evening when you are not meeting. I am afraid that some day he will also start singing some tune."

His friend looked contented at this development and started singing the requested one.

Music and fun flowed endlessly between the three of them.

All was almost fine till one day like a thunderbolt he got the notice from his company that he would have to look for another job. Like the old days, his friend desperately wanted to assuage his frustration.

"Look. Don't feel so low. Don't be anxious so much. I know you have a lot of money in the bank but still I would like you to remember that I am

always there. I have no family and the salary is more than enough for me. I don't mind spending money for all three of us. You can pay me back with interest once you are back in action. I promise, I shall maintain a detailed record of what I shall spend for you."

He smiled faintly, "I know you are there but I have enough for some more time. When required I shall tell you, and by the way... don't keep that record. I don't think I would bother to pay you back ever. Just recall how many cigarettes you borrowed from me in the college days."

The heaviness of the conversation diluted immediately but the brooding air stayed. One evening, his friend wanted to meet him outside the house in the absence of his wife.

"I understand you are planning to use your wife's ornaments! Don't do that."

"But it's not me who wanted to use them."

"I know ... last night you discussed all these right in front of me. Don't take them. Just slog for some more time. You will get a better job."

"But... but... neither do I want to take them. I know they are very close to her heart."

"I have come across many women who never forgive their husbands for this reason. It's a common practice to use the ornaments of the house. But I strongly advise you not to do that."

"I know there is some sense in what you are saying but I want to start a business!"

"Business!"

His friend fell silent and tried to assimilate the idea.

So... he was in business. The business started with a jerk and success started rolling in at an unexpected pace. His friend was ecstatic. He was getting back his lost dignity and his wife was confused. She suddenly discovered that the homely husband was barely able to devote any time in the house. Even if he was at home his mind stayed somewhere else. She complained one day, "Earlier, life was better. Now you are always busy!"

"I can't help it. Earlier I used to help others make money; and now I make money for myself. Every penny I generate gives me a sense of achievement. I can't slow down at this stage."

After a long gap of one week his friend called him one day when he was busy in a meeting bargaining on a payment term, "I've got a new collection of Ghazals. Let's listen to them together in the evening. I promise you would love them."

"Ah...I am busy right now. I shall call you back."

The line snapped. His friend never found him busy enough in the past to refuse a conversation. In fact during the college days, he used to be the only student who always had time and still obtained bright results. It was a shock for his friend. He had never been so curt. The whole morning, noon and evening went by but his call never came.

In the evening, his friend knocked on his door and his wife said, "He is yet to come. Today he is dining out with a client and will come home late."

Their relaxed evening sessions almost came to an end. He started earning a lot and craved for more. One day he shifted from that small two bed room apartment to a bungalow nearby. He paid a fortune for that.

"I understand that you are earning a lot but don't you think you've spent too much on that?" chided his friend.

"Hmm...from your point of view it's correct but then I have a status. Sometimes, some business associates visit my house and I can't show them that I live in a dingy shack like that!" His friend was surprised at him. He had changed immensely. His involvement in the affairs of the house decreased; his wife started becoming unhappy by every day. They often argued and fought over small matters. In the mean time the child was born. But nothing could bring his attention back to the family. The household was slowly dipping into a brooding dumbness. Except for the occasional laughter and cry of the new born baby there was no expression of joy or excitement. His friend kept

meeting him occasionally whenever he was available at home at earthly hours. But their music evenings and happy chitchats had no room in the interaction any more. Whenever he spoke, he spoke of business deals and local politics. One day his friend asked him, "Your needs are fulfilled now. Why are you running like that after money oblivious to every other aspect of life? You are doing something that has lost its purpose. Now it's just the habit that's driving you. I think you can slow down and look around...you have run too far too fast...you have left your loved ones behind."

He replied smugly, "These are excuses for those who are tired of running. You will not understand the passion. You don't have it. I have a mission unlike you and I am driving towards that."

His friend understood that he was not to be convinced. In fact this statement hurt his friend somewhere. His arrogance started demeaning others lately. The familiar identity was slowly fading out and a new personality was crystallizing.

His friend and his wife never spoke about the unwelcome changes in his character but silently bore the loss of each other. One evening his friend called him over phone, "Am I invited tomorrow?"

"I don't understand... You don't need an invitation for knocking on your neighbour's door."

"Well...you are busy now a days...so! And it's not a dry run. I mean, am I invited for a spiritual dinner in the evening?"

"I am not sure...I might have to catch a flight tomorrow evening...let's see. But there's no occasion!"

"There were actually no occasions in the past for such evenings. Anyway... we shall talk tomorrow."

The line went dead. He did not like people talking in riddles. He had little time for small talk.

The next morning he was going through the news paper and sipping his tea when the bell rang. His wife was busy mixing milk in the feeding bottle for the baby. The maid servant also was engaged in some other activity. He waited for some time for someone else to respond to the door bell but when nobody came forward he himself got up from the sofa to open the door. Right at that moment, the telephone started ringing. He was in a dilemma about what to attend first. After a moment's deliberation, he quickly went and opened the door. There was something strange but he did not ask any question. He just indicated the guest to wait there and went back to the telephone to receive the call.

"Hallo,"

"Don't be surprised. Look at the calendar. Pay for the flowers. I have not paid for you...at least this much you have to do." The line snapped. It was his friend!

He quickly looked at the calendar and immediately it flashed in his mind that this was his marriage anniversary. He had totally forgotten. His wife was still busy. He went back to the door. The boy was still waiting there with a huge bouquet of flowers.

He quickly paid for the bouquet and asked the boy to wait there. The boy waited. He called his wife, "Can you see who's there at the door?"

His wife grudgingly went to attend the guest at the door. As she found the huge bouquet standing on the floor half blocking the view of the small boy who brought it, she was almost happy that her husband did not forget the day yet. And this little mischief on her husband's part made her smile.

"So...I remember this day!" said her husband with a broad smile.

"I see that! How did it happen...it's unbelievable! I thought you were too busy for such silly things."

He called his friend and said, "I think I should invite you in the evening. I have cancelled my flight today."

"Hmm...I am coming."

They celebrated that evening together. Efforts were made to simulate the past but the enthusiasm was missing.

Then one day the other woman clouded his life and eventually his wife came to know of the affair. Their marital life went for a toss. Every morning, noon and night turned bitter and vengeful. He often did not come back home at night and did not bother to give any explanation. Once, he did not return for three days at a stretch and when he was back he went straight to his friend's place for a couple of drinks. They spent the evening drinking. His friend did not ask him even once about where he had been for three days but tried to channel the conversation towards some other matters that had little significance.

He wanted to speak about himself and said at some point of time, "I have reason of being disloyal. This lady has brought in some fresh air in my life."

His friend stayed silent for a long moment and then said diffidently, "Don't you think you are destroying a beautiful family? I think you are simply allowing yourself a derangement."

"What's wrong? I have never asked my wife to leave me. I just want to live. She is not concerned about me anymore. She only wants loyalty at the cost of nothing."

His friend said nothing and tried to change the subject. He was visibly upset that he could not garner any support. Anyway, the crack was there and after this the crack was wider. He quickly finished his drinks and left for home with a gloomy face. There was nothing but hostility awaiting him there.

"Where have you been for the past three days?" charged his wife.

"I am not a jobless vagabond loitering here and there. Don't question me in that tone. I hate that."

"You hate anything and everything about me. It's not new. But tell me where have you been?"

"I had a series of meetings and stayed in the company guest house during the nights. Anything else?"

"No. Thanks."

The conversation reached a dead end.

The next morning, his friend knocked on his door on his way to office and his wife opened the door.

"Here is this bunch of papers he left at my place by mistake. Could you give it to him?"

"Yes, sure."

His wife looked at the folded bunch of papers and something prompted her to open the folds. The papers turned out to be a bunch of nicely printed bills from a five star hotel in the city. Her mind started racing. She checked the dates and the names of the occupants. The names turned out to be of him and the other woman. They had stayed for three days in a presidential suite of the posh hotel. Even the food bills were attached as a reference. She rushed to the study room where her husband was looking into some files. She banged the door open and barged in.

"You bloody cheat! You liar! Look here!" she threw the sheaf of papers on the floor in front of her husband. He immediately realized the blunder as soon as he took a quick glance at the bills strewn all over the floor.

The day started with a cynical and vengeful fight. After a while he left the house and went to the office. Life seemed quite unworthy of living at that point of time. He had often considered the option of asking for a divorce but immediately the innocent face of his son crushed his plan.

As soon as he reached office, he picked up the phone and in a fit of anger dialed the number of his friend, "What is your problem?"

"Meaning?"

"Why did you have to come and flash the hotel bill to my wife?"

"Oh my God! Believe me I never knew it was a hotel bill. I did not even open the folded papers. They were lying on the floor and I just collected them while cleaning the table after you left my house last night."

"Come on! Tell me the truth. Why did you do this?"

"I am sorry! But I had no idea... but what is wrong with that?"

"You don't know what you mean! It's too much now. Could you please mind your own business from this day onwards instead of interfering in my family? I am tired and sick of your concerns and meddling."

His friend did not answer.

He was boiling with demonic rage, "Are you listening?"

"Yes, I am. I shall stay away. Thanks!"

They hung up.

Slowly as the days went by his irritation was mitigated. By evening he was slowly realizing that the harshness with which he spoke to his friend was a mistake. The next day, he went to apologize for his behavior but that apology did not go well it seemed. The delicate bond of the old relationship was damaged. His friend still remained in touch with his family but maintained a distinct gap from him. Though they spoke and laughed yet the frankness went missing for ever. He never spoke about his life to his friend because he knew he would not support his reasoning and logic. Since the whole world seemed to look at his extramarital affair as a heinous offence towards his good family, he turned hostile to the whole world. A general hatred and arrogance symbolized his character. He knew that his friend could see through his hardened façade and touch his vulnerability. He took special care to hide his inner dilemma and susceptibility from his friend's notice.

The telephone was ringing for the third time and he jolted back from his reverie. He decided to take the call and pressed the talk button. But instantly the screen went blank. There was no battery! He dialed the reception and requested for a mobile charger. In few minutes time there was a charger in his hand.

He plugged the mobile with the charger and it started charging. He wondered if he would return the call but on second thoughts he dropped the idea. He left the cell phone charging in the room and staggered out slamming the door behind him. There were a number of cabs waiting for passengers just outside the hotel. He boarded one of them and asked for the ATM.

From a distance itself he realized that the ATM had started to work because there was a small queue. Finally, he pushed his card in and drew a load of cash. He was not going to take any more chances.

He asked the taxi driver to drive to the highway. The taxi driver swung around in surprise, "Now! To the highway!"

"Yes! You heard it right. Let's go. I shall pay. Don't worry."

The taxi zoomed into the dark night in the direction of the highway.

"Where are you, bloody cheat?" he yelled at the man when he saw his car still parked in front of the shed with one wheel missing.

Initially, there was no response. Actually the boy had gone to fetch some help from wherever he could get any. The man was lying half conscious on his bed. The loud shouting from the road made him startle. The man tried to decipher what was being stated. As he recognized the source of such angry yelling, he forced himself to get up and finally stood on the ground. Taking support of the objects around, the man somehow managed to come out of the shed.

"You crook! You did not even touch my car over the past six hours! You thought I would not be able to bring any money? Listen I am not a beggar like you...You don't know who I am!" he shouted on top of his voice.

The man stared at him trying to grasp the situation.

"No ... no... I just could not do it. I have been sleeping all the time. I am so sorry...but...but you are still angry!" The man tried to smile.

"Don't show that stupid smile of yours. It snaps all the control I have on my temper. I know why you did not do the job. You thought that I was another wandering vagabond who went on scouting for money vainly." As he spoke he became angrier by every word.

"Huh! You are mistaken. It's so strange that my smile did not work on you! See…I told you before that when I smile at the sun the sun becomes bearable. If I don't curse the heat, it does not curse me…see…what has happened…there is no heat now…the blinding glow is not scorching our eyes any more…see…they are no more our enemies…see…" the man said something more but the words came out garbled from his mouth.

He looked at the shadowy figure of the man in disgust and uttered spitefully. "Either you are completely mad or you are a cunning bugger…listen…I am leaving now but will be right back in the morning. If I don't find this car with all four wheels, I shall kill you right here."

Suddenly the boy rushed back from somewhere and found him shouting loudly at the man. The boy watched the situation for a few seconds and growled at him. He said, "Just get lost from here right now. He is sick. I am running around for help and you are shouting at him like this. Just get lost, I say."

"Hey … you silly boy…just shut up okay…one slap and all your teeth will vanish," he said sneeringly.

The boy quickly picked up a large stone from the ground and made a gesture of throwing it at him. He was suddenly scared and quickly went back to the taxi.

While the taxi was driving away he shouted again and announced the name of the hotel where he was put up and warned, "I want my car in the morning … otherwise I shall show you…"

The boy slowly put down the stone on the dusty ground and led the man back to his bed.

Once in the bed, the man looked at the ceiling with half closed delirious eyes and said "I must fit that tyre. Let me take some rest for few minutes and then I shall get to work."

The boy pleaded with him not to get up but after half an hour or so the man somehow managed to rise to his feet and started working on the tyre.

He inserted the new tube into the tyre and filled it with air. Finally, he picked up the new tyre from the ground and went to the front left wheel of the car to do the fitting.

In a few minutes the tyre was in its place. The man removed the jack and staggered back to his bed as if in a hypnotic trance.

He lay on the bed again in a delirium.

Back in hotel, he went straight to the bar. The bar was closing. The tired slogged out waiters were cleaning up the place and putting the things back in the store.

He slumped onto a chair and bellowed, "One large whisky...my favorite brand please...and you must know that...I don't need mention...fast!"

"Sorry, Sir. The bar is closed now," one of the waiters said curtly.

"What? Closed? Nothing is closed for me...come on...everything was closed for me till one hour back...but not now...bring my whisky."

"Sorry, Sir. We don't serve any drinks after one in the morning."

He glared at the waiter.

She found the white horse

She was standing on top of a mountain. She had never seen such an arid and wild landscape. There were plenty of shriveled trees with their grayish trunks rooted to the parched ground. There were cracks on the rough soil running from one end to the other like poisonous snakes. The air was still and carried an odor of staleness. The sky on top of her head was black. No stars glittered anywhere. The moon appeared to be a hazy ball of yellow light almost smudged with the dull blackness as if it was another sky...another moon...another night. She was standing at the peak of the mountain waiting for the prince to come. The prince was coming from some faraway place riding a white horse with wings. She looked down at the bottom of the mountain and saw her father like a tiny dot. He was calling her pet name desperately. His voice was faint. Still she could see that her father was standing there at the foot of the mountain and pleading with her to come down from the peak, begging her not to go away with the prince on the white horse with wings.

She was listening but was not convinced. The prince would come and take her away from that deadness flying through the dark night.

Her father was speaking in supplication, "Look...if you come down carefully, I shall get you red and yellow balloons you always loved. I shall get you a box full of chocolates. As many ice creams you want, I shall bring for you. Your teddy bear? You remember that? I still have it with me...don't you want that back. See... this teddy has not slept or eaten anything after you left home...come...please come down...I shall buy you a dozen crayons and drawing books. Don't you want that tri cycle you wanted but I never bought. Come and I shall get you one...I shall sing you that song you always wanted to hear before sleeping...you just come down from there. Please don't go with that prince..." her father was almost crying. She listened but did not move. Far into the black nothingness, the white horse of the prince was faintly visible. The flapping of the wings was almost audible. She stretched her eyes to get a clearer view of the prince. He was bringing something with him; a bag full of dazzling dreams! She saw the beautiful dreams. A magnificent palace made of milk white marbles stood resolutely in the horizon with open arms coaxing her to walk into it. Thousand candles sparkled with flickering flames around it illuminating the dark night. A chariot with seven horses waited at the gate of the palace just for her to step into the carriage. In a flicker of an eyelid the prince arrived and his white horse with large wings was standing in front of her. The prince stretched his hand for her to hold. She took his hand and climbed onto the back of the horse. The horse was starting to move and she could still hear her father's frantic pleading, "Please don't go with him...come down from there..."

She did not pay any heed to that and sat on the horse's back clutching the prince. The horse started its journey. It started to run and then the pace increased. Finally it was air-born. The mountain peak vanished from view and then she was racing through the dark nothingness around her. Her father's voice faded into oblivion as the horse flew farther and farther into the thick emptiness. The horse was now flying faster and faster. She could feel the pace. The horse suddenly entered into a fog of thick grey cloud and then there was a violent jerk. She tried to grab the prince to brace herself against the horse but the prince seemed to have vanished abruptly and she ended up clasping a void. The jerks became intense one after the other and she could no longer hold onto the back of the horse. In a fit of fear she bent forward and toppled from the horse back. She screamed in fear but nothing could stop her falling. She darted towards the ground at blistering pace. She fell and fell. It seemed to be a bottomless pit dragging her deep into its womb from where no hand could reach her for rescue. She wanted to cry but no sound escaped her lips. She was falling...just waiting helplessly to hit the hard merciless ground and smash into a lump of blood and flesh. After an endless suffocating fall through a dark tunnel of nothingness suddenly she hit the end! But to her surprise it did not hurt her at all; instead it was as if a soft cushion that held her with care and affection. She opened her eyes and looked at the person whose arms held her so tenderly...she realized it was her father. Tears of happiness rolled out of her eyes...she clasped his neck...and then the ringing sound of the telephone penetrated her dreaming consciousness. She lay still in her bed for some more time. The telephone was ringing adamantly refusing to give up. She slowly sat up and looked at the arrogant machine. Slowly the haze cleared from her mind and she realized the uncanny incoming call could not be a normal one. The larger hand of the wall clock was about to reach one in the morning! Who could call her at that hour! She rose to her feet and approached the table to receive the call.

An alien voice floated from the other end. She was immediately apprehensive and asked for more clarification about the identity of the caller and the purpose of the call.

The dead end

There was a commotion. A huge crowd had gathered around the place. All lights were switched on immediately.

"It's all over!"

"Are you sure?"

"What a stupid question!"

"No…it's strange!"

"What's strange about it?"

"Just like that?"

"Why? You expect a grand ceremony or something before this happened?"

"You mean the reason is as simple as you said?"

"Yes, it is. Actually you rarely come across such reasons because most of us suffer from malnutrition instead of…! Of course these are the reasons for the others getting less than they deserve"

"Don't be philosophical…call the police."

"Shall we try the cell phone?"

"For what? Police is toll free … our hotel land line is good enough"

"Come on! Not for the call charges…don't be foolish. I am talking about some familiar numbers"

"You have a point. Let's try!"

"Look here...I think we should check the address book."

"Yes. Just scroll...yes...yes...stop... stop there! Ahh...go back a little."

"Which one?"

"Home...try that number."

They dialed the number listed under the name: "Home."

The night fades away when eyes sleep

His wife was fast asleep in her bed clasping her baby boy close to her bosom. With the loud ringing sound of the telephone, her son stirred slightly within the confinement of her arms. The ringing sound penetrated her sleeping brain and she blinked her eyes a few times to drive away the sleep. As her mind cleared, she stared at the telephone and thought it must be her husband. She looked at the clock. It was well past midnight. The frustration with which she went to sleep was still hurting as a fresh wound. He refused to take her call few hours back He must have been busy devouring the body of that witch. Now as he was through, he was calling back. She decided to give it back and did not get up from her bed. Her son was still being disturbed by the ring. She placed her palm on his ear and embraced him even tighter to offer the warmth of her motherly softness. The phone kept ringing till the last breath and then suddenly fell silent. There was no more noise in the room. She slept with her son, coiled into a single piece of love, affection and tenderness. Life sailed through the cold silence of the dark night.

The dead end

"No one is taking the call."

"Okay...just try the number of the last received call...may be that might help us."

"Oh!! See that number stored with the name, "Sweet heart"! Poor fellow."

"Unfortunate wife!"

"Let's dial."

"Well...this time there might be some luck it seems. It's ringing!"

"Good! Tell the wife what happened."

"Hallo..."

The end is not dead!

"Madam…there is something about your husband."

"Who?"

"Your husband…ah…well…Are you the wife of Mr.…?"

"That's immaterial…who are you? What about him?"

"Okay…he just…"

She listened intently whatever was narrated from the other end. During this span neither her expression changed nor her eyes blinked. As soon as their short message was conveyed, she put the phone down without any warning.

She stood there transfixed to the spot for a long moment and then suddenly got back to consciousness. As if she knew exactly what she had to do. With a determined gesture full of conviction, she swiftly changed her dress and quickly ran the comb through her unkempt hair. As the hair looked regular, she coiled the long bunch of hair into a bun at the back of her neck and quickly clipped the bunch of hair to prevent it from falling over the back. Then, she went to the living room and took out the purse from the drawer. There were a few notes in the bag. She counted them roughly and in an unconscious reflex she collected two keys from the hook that hung on the wall. As she was about to leave the room, she happened to notice the two keys in her hand. She looked at the key with a large black head and pondered something, "No...she does not require that any more.". She slowly went near the wall and hung the key back on the wall. She walked out of the room and closed the door behind her.

In a minute she was in the courtyard.

She walked past the series of cars parked at one side near the boundary wall. Her own car was also parked there neatly. She walked towards the state transport bus terminus. The terminus was not far away and there was bus service all over the night. She went to the staff room and asked if there were a bus during the night for the small town in the middle of the highway. The half asleep old man nodded, "Yes"

She went to the terminus and checked the number of the bus that was supposed to leave in ten minutes. The bus was empty at that time of the night. She occupied a window seat at the centre of the bus. After ten minutes sharp the engine of the bus raved with a vibration. The silence of the night seemed to break into a million pieces as the bus started to move with all its metallic parts in grind.

And then tears giggled…

The boy was sitting at the head of the bed. The man was staring at the ceiling with dreamy eyes.

"I knew it would work and it worked. See…the stars are back…the ones I lost when I was a child like you. The wind never ran its passionate finger through my hair the whole day. It was arguing with me as I complained. But see…now the wind is running all over my body. Oh! I feel great!

I was wrong…nothing goes. The sun did not go but only went to fetch some more light for me…he told me before leaving this afternoon. The rain! Oh! I am such a fool ... I forgot…the rain even told me that it was leaving for a while just to gather some more news for me…she knows that I love to talk and listen…In fact nothing goes…neither shall I go anywhere…how can I run away from myself…see…how comfortable I am…all of them are pampering me as if I am a small baby…oh…I have never seen all of them together…the morning sun…the sky full of stars…the drizzling rain…the winter breeze…the flashing lightning…all of them…all of them…I feel so much better…like a butterfly in thin air…"

The voice of the man slowly started fading out into the solemn silence of the night and the boy watched him perplexed. The boy knew that the man was happy…peaceful and completely devoid of any physical trouble. He was indeed like a butterfly in the thin crisp air...

The voice slowly came to a stop and the boy placed his ears on the chest of the man to listen if there was any heart beat left. Surprisingly, he could not hear any heart beat but he heard the gurgling sound of a waterfall...chirping of birds and rustle of wind blowing through leaves of verdant trees. The boy knew that there was nothing to be sad.

After a few hours, the sun indeed appeared in the eastern horizon. The boy slowly got up from the side of the bed where the man's body was still lying motionless.

The car was ready to be driven away by the owner.

The boy started walking towards the hill station. He could have taken a bus but he was not aware where the pouch of money was kept. So, he started to walk.

After almost an hour of walking through the hills he arrived near the hotel. There was a tense and curious crowd around the hotel building. The boy tried to guess what was happening there. There was also a police vehicle stationed on the road. Without any clue, the boy diffidently walked towards the hotel entrance. There was a hushed buzz among the people.

"What is the matter?" asked the boy.

"One guest died last night in the bar," said an excited voice.

The boy was curious but he could not afford to spend much time there because he had to go back to the shed.

He further asked, "Is it a murder? Who was it?"

"It's a man of middle age. He checked in last noon and the hotel people said that he ordered loads of food and a lot of drinks to his room. After consuming those, he went somewhere at night and finally came back at one o clock and went straight to the bar. The bar was closed and he raised hell of a chaos for more drinks. He was already dead drunk by that time. They were telling the police and I overheard. They say that he was pretty offensive and was waving a bunch of notes in the air and shouting that he could purchase the whole bar with that. In that chaos suddenly he collapsed on the ground and seemed to have died almost immediately. There is a doctor in the hotel. The doctor checked him and said that he had died out of over-eating and cold. He seemed to have been roaming around in the sun during the day and suddenly exposed himself to the chill of air-conditioner for a long time."

"But where is the body...can I see?" the boy asked anxiously.

By that time the ambulance had already lifted the body and was carrying it out of the building to load into the van. There was still a bunch of notes held tightly in the grip of the dead body.

The boy watched with pensive eyes the owner of the car being loaded into the ambulance. On its way the stretcher was rocked by a few jerks and the grip loosened a little resulting in a few notes slipping out. It seemed that nobody really noticed the event but the boy did. He did not leave the place and kept waiting till the ambulance and the police were gone. There was not much mystery in the death. Hence police did not spend much time there.

As the crowd was thinning out, the boy stealthily lifted the fallen slice of the bunch of notes that was still lying on the ground. He tucked the bunch in his pocket and started walking back towards the highway. As he was leaving the place suddenly a female voice stopped him. He looked around and found a young lady standing at a distance from the crowd by the side of the road. He stared at her with curiosity and the lady repeated her question, "What are you going to do with that money?"

The boy was nervous and said defensively, "What money? There is no money!"

The lady said impassively, "Don't hide. I have seen you taking the money that fell on the ground."

The boy remained silent now and could not look into her eyes. After some time the boy asked, "Did you know him?"

The lady said, "How does it matter. We know everyone or nobody."

"I don't understand."

"You are too clean to understand that. But that money you have taken would make you understand such things. By the way, why did you come here? It looks like you had something to do with him."

"Yes. His car is parked at our shed. The tyre was punctured yesterday and we had to repair it. I came to tell him that his car was ready."

"I see."

"I feel you knew him. Would you like to take this money?"

"No. I don't want that money. What do you plan to do with that money, by the way?"

"There is a nice food mall near our repair shop. I will go there and eat all the delicious food available in their kitchen. I'll sit at one of the tables and place my order like everyone else does."

"After that?"

"After that...after that...I don't know...my stomach will be full and I will be happy like everybody else."

"But that's for an hour or two! Then you will be hungry again!"

"That's true. I shall eat again..."

"Till your money lasts, I guess."

"Hmm..."

"Let's assume...you have unlimited money..."

"Then I shall keep on eating."

"And getting hungry again after an hour or two..."

"And eating again..."

"So...you see...this would be like a ping pong ball bouncing up and down... your pleasure will vanish either because your money will finish or your hunger will be consumed. Either way your pleasure is bound to disappear into thin air...isn't it?"

"That's correct!"

"Hence...this money will actually never bring you internal satisfaction."

"But then...I am hungry!"

"I know that you are hungry...so go ahead and buy food with that money."

"Will you take the car? It's ready."

"No. I will not. I don't need that any more. You can keep it with you as long as you can. Only make sure that you drive the car instead of the car driving you. If that happens, you are doomed because the roads are very wild and you will be taken for a ride. Any time some dark abyss will gulp you into its bottomless pit."

The boy stared at her totally confused and finally decided to move. The woman said, "Wish you all the best!" And she set off on her journey towards the nearest bus stand.

Once on the highway, he met the morning breeze flowing swiftly though the space. The heat seemed to have disappeared somewhere. The dryness in the air seemed to have softened down considerably. There were some flakes of cloud in the sky. The parched landscape seemed to have turned relatively greener than yesterday. Suddenly he was conscious of the bunch of notes sticking in his pocket. He pulled out the bunch and looked at it. Immediately the sight of the endless winding highway fizzled out and the vision of a wild giant adorned with glittering gems and jewels, savagely eating gory flesh of some live animal flashed from nowhere. The boy was prickled with extreme fear and disgust. The giant was eating like a maniac. Dazzling glow of light flooded his formidable countenance. Having eaten all that was in his hand ... he started howling for more...he started scrambling everything around him and finally when he failed to locate anything more, he started biting his own hand furiously, spilling blood and rotten flesh all around.

The boy trembled in fear and the bunch of notes slipped out of his hand. Since they were loose, the notes disintegrated and the leaves started floating away in the air. The boy suddenly jolted back to consciousness and was relieved to get back to his familiar highway and morning breeze. He was about to run after the floating notes but a gust of wind unruffled his hair and kissed his cheeks tenderly reminding him of something else. It was the face of the man lying in the shed, steeped in serenity, peace and happiness. The man looked happy for eternity dissolved into the unfathomable blue of the sky, sizzled in the summer heat and now sleeping in the cloud ready to visit the earth as rain drops, smiling with the sun to flash a dazzling welcome in the morning...

The boy let the notes float away aimlessly and held out his young hand. The wind accepted his hand and led him towards a happy journey like a butterfly in the thin air.